MANNEQUIN

MANNEQUIN is a work of fiction. The events and characters that are described are imaginary and are not intended to refer to specific places or living persons.

MANNEQUIN
A series: Book 4

V.M. JACKSON

Chapter 1

"Once upon a time"

Smoke filled the air and fire blazed through nearby trees as Quinn drove her black BMW through the bomb massacred church parking lot. Shaking her head in a frantic, she tried to calm herself down as best as she could.

"You're *okay*, Quinn, just relax and breathe," she coached. "Slow, deep breaths. That's it. *Slow...deep* brea-" veering quickly to the left, she dodged a child's blown off foot. Quinn screamed, immediately slamming on her brakes as she began to hyperventilate. "Oh my goodness, what kind of *evil* would do something like this?" As a world-renowned psychologist, Quinn had just about seen and heard it all. *Or so she thought.* She'd dealt with angry wives who, after being victims of infidelity, murdered their husbands, the mistresses, the children, and the family pet. She witnessed patients come to the end of their sanity and commit suicide right in her office. She knew some of the best lawyers who could advocate for and advise criminals, but stood in her presence in mid panic attack, in search of someone to advocate for them. Eight months ago she'd met a Doctor, William Goodrich, who performed surgery on Eden to remove a bullet from her skull. He was an attractive forty-five-year-old man who was absolutely smitten with Quinn. She reintroduced him to Christ and resurrected the faith he lost after his mother suffered a grueling death at the hands of cancer.

Weeks later, Dr. Goodrich began attending her church with his fiancée. He came to hear the Pastor preach, but he also came to eye down the Pastor's wife. Dr. Goodrich wanted to remain faithful to his fiancée, but he couldn't get Quinn off of his mind. Her beauty and grace was something out of a fairy tale, and he couldn't stop himself from thinking about her. Her innocent smile and poise had given him a new lease on life, and he began fantasizing about what it would be like to be Quinn's husband. Eventually, his fantasies had shifted into a full-blown obsession. Dr. Goodrich began attending bible studies because he knew Quinn would be there, and he joined the security ministry to escort her around when she needed to preach at other churches. He even went so far as to fake a depression and signed himself up for her therapy sessions. After long hours of healing the sick and raising the dead in the emergency room, the demands of work had begun to take a toll on Dr. Goodrich. He'd go home to a fiancée that couldn't cook, wouldn't clean, and always needed something from him.

Quinn's encouraging words, soft voice, yet powerful presence became just what Dr. Goodrich needed. Eventually, he switched his therapy sessions from once a month, to once a week. The more he saw of Quinn, the less he wanted to see of his fiancée. He'd become so mentally addicted to Quinn that he would go home and stare at his fiancée in utter disgust because she didn't measure up. After a few months, it became evident that Dr. Goodrich had fallen in love with a woman who belonged to someone else. He grew emotionally damaged and depressed, *for real* this time. As he became more double-minded and unstable, his work at the hospital began to suffer. He made senseless mistakes in the operating room resulting in the unfortunate deaths of healthy patients. Still, to the public eye, Dr. William Goodrich was one of the best surgeons in Virginia.

Weeks later, he was nationally recognized after performing a successful, ten-hour brain surgery on one of his patients. He walked up to the podium arm an arm with his fiancée to accept his award, wishing so badly that it was Quinn by his side. He felt guilty and perverted for allowing his thoughts to get the best of him. He warred with himself and beat himself up about it all night long. The next day, he walked into Quinn's office for his appointment with a shotgun and blew his head off. Quinn screamed as blood and brain matter sprayed all over her face. Collapsed on her office floor lay the splattered remains of Virginia's top brain surgeon; William, D. Goodrich. *What a mess.* Throughout Quinn's ten years as a psychologist, she'd crossed paths with serial killers, rapists and child molesters, but nothing, absolutely *nothing* could have prepared her for this. *A bomb in the church.* Her thoughts raced over and over, braking on the same statement. She clutched her steering wheel until her knuckles turned ashen white and her hands trembled like the ground during an earthquake. Through the smoke, she could see the welcome sign of her church, well, *what was left of it*:

"Tabernacle Church of God in Christ.

Because Maury isn't the only place to find your father."

Tears fell from Quinn's helpless eyes as she remembered her first encounter at Tabernacle. Her mother, Dr. Olivia Gray, and Andre's mother, First Lady Guilda Bentley, met at Miss Ruby's hair salon one early Saturday morning. Olivia sat under the dryer scanning a magazine while Miss Ruby put the finishing touches on Guilda's French roll.

"Ruby, you are the queen of the curling iron," Guilda held a mirror up to her hair, admiring her beautiful updo.

"Oh good, you like it?" Ruby smiled. "This was my first time trying the French roll. My husband and I traveled to Paris for the first time and saw one of their Cirque du Soleil shows. Honey, those women were amazing, and their hair was rolled and pinned up with all sorts of accessories at the top and the sides."

"I agree, those Parisian women really know how to put on a show, right?" Olivia lowered her magazine and chimed in. "My husband and I went for our anniversary last year and we were blown away."

"I was blown away by their hair," Ruby replied. "I waited three hours after the show was over for one of the girls to exit the building so I could ask her the type of style it was. She told me it was a Franchesca French roll. She let me look at it to see how it was done. As soon as I came back to the States, I grabbed my mannequin head and started to practice but I couldn't get the gel to slick the edges like I wanted, so when I did yours I experimented with the curls flowing out of the top."

"It looks beautiful," Guilda stood up, admiring herself in the full-length mirror behind her, "The women at church will love this, and I'm going to send them straight to you."

"Too bad my hair is close to being finished," Olivia tisked, "Ruby Doo, you *must* put me down for that French roll during my next visit."

"I most certainly will," Ruby confirmed. Guilda reached into her purse and pulled out three twenty-dollar bills, handing it to Ruby."

"Oh no, this is way too much money," Ruby's eyes

widened, "I only charge thirty dollars for a wash and style."

"Consider it an extra thank you," Guilda winked, "and put me on the schedule for two weeks from today, will you?" As the three of them conversed, ten-year-old Andre and Mannequin sat by the children's bookshelf arguing.

"Can you move? I'm trying to read," Quinn fussed, annoyed at Andre for breathing down her neck as she read through a book.

"Can you hurry up and turn the page? I'm trying to read too," Andre fussed back.

"You cannot read while I'm reading. Get your own book."

"Well I don't want to get my own book, I want to read while your reading, so hurry up and turn the page so *we* can finish the story." Furrowing her eyebrows at the tall, dark-skinned boy, Quinn clamped the book shut.

"Well, I can't finish reading until you stop breathing your alligator breath on my neck." Andre snatched the book from Quinn's hands. "Hey, give that back."

"Make me, *weirdo*," Andre shot back. Quinn tried reaching for the book, but Andre dodged away from her hands. "Go back to whatever planet gave you those scary looking eyes."

"I got my eyes from my mother, *thank* you," Quinn replied with sass.

"She must be married to the devil then because they look evil," he laughed.

"And I assume you got your skin color from *your* black, crispy mother?" Quinn hissed.

"I'm rubber, you're glue, whatever bounces off of me, *sticks to you*," Andre teased.

"Give me back my book!" Quinn stood up. Andre

stuck out his tongue, hilariously mocking Quinn until she'd finally had enough. Rolling up her sleeves, she grabbed Andre by his feet and slid him out of the chair. Andre's arms flung into the air, causing the book to fall flat on his face.

"Let me go, weirdo," he protested, but Quinn didn't listen. She dragged him up and down the salon floor like a rag doll.

"Mannequin!" Olivia gasped, jumping out of her seat, nearly taking the hairdryer with her.

"Andre, baby," Guilda hollered, watching her only child being swept across the floor. Both of the women rushed to break up the embarrassing scene.

"What *brats,*" Ruby mumbled under her breath. Guilda and Olivia became good friends after that. Outside of her best friend Sophia, Olivia hadn't really made friends in her hometown. She'd just started her own practice and worked many nights in the emergency room at the Sentara Virginia Beach Hospital until her clientele built up. Guilda was a breath of fresh air compared to Sophia. Sophia had dropped out of college during her senior year after she fell pregnant a second time with her daughter, Joanna. She ended up marrying her big shot, investment broker husband, Joseph and was trying to adjust to life as a stay at home mom. Guilda had a Ph.D. in Biology. On days when she wasn't serving in ministry, she worked as a scientist on a Naval Base. Olivia's love of medicine, paired with Guilda's love of science drew a close-knit friendship filled with afternoon lunches and play dates with their children.

Quinn and Andre tolerated one another for the sake of their parents but argued like cats and dogs. One day, Guilda suggested Olivia and her family come to church, and Olivia did just that. That next Sunday, Olivia and her husband, the honorable Judge Steven Gray, and Quinn pulled into the five-acre parking lot of Tabernacle Church of God in Christ. Gazing out the window, they all marveled at the architecture, craftsmanship, and construction of the English Tudor, Victorian-styled church.

"This looks like a castle, momma," Quinn looked through the car window with wide eyes.

"Maybe it used to be, once upon a time," Olivia shook her head in awe, wondering how anyone could build something so beautiful. The church was three hundred and sixty-five feet long, and one hundred and sixty-five feet tall. Its two towers extended two hundred and thirty-seven feet into the sky. The Gray family exited their car and walked toward the main entry that etched two big doors within its frame. Above the entrance lie an exquisite stained-glass rose window imported from Europe. Everything was covered by a gabled roof with stone lintels, sills at the ends, and topped with a cross. There were poinsettias and azaleas everywhere they looked. The parking lot was made of smooth white stone so flawless, it looked like an entryway to heaven.

"I'll bet there's a princess locked away at the very top, and a fire breathing dragon blocking the entrance to her," Quinn said.

"You certainly are a hopeless romantic," Judge Steven chuckled, "just like your mother." He reached for his wife's hand as Olivia turned to him and smiled, planting a kiss on his cheek.

"I've passed this place all the time during my Sunday morning runs," Steven said, "I could always hear the amazing music playing from inside. I'm excited to see all the voice behind the melody."

"I hear the choir is to die for," Olivia gawked.

"Guilda told me the choir director directs national choirs down in Georgia. They pay his airfare and hotel fees just to come here every week and direct."

"Wow," Steven nodded, impressed. The sound of Guilda's name caused Quinn to stop walking.

"Guilda? Andre's mother? We have to hang out with those *freaks* again?" Quinn furrowed.

"*Mannequin*?" Olivia froze, her lips parted in shock as she clutched her chest, "What on earth- where did you learn to speak so loosely?

"I'm not speaking loosely, I'm being honest. I don't like that we always have to hang out with them. Can't you find some *new* friends while you're waiting for Mrs. Sophia to get her marriage together?" Olivia gasped, sending a back-handed slap straight into in her daughter's face. It was the first time she'd ever physically scolded her. Judge Steven raised an eyebrow. He had no idea what had gotten into his sweet daughter, or his wife.

"You watch your mouth and stay out of grown folks business, young lady," Olivia pointed in her face. Quinn turned bright red, as tears of embarrassment streamed down her cheeks. The entire left side of her face stung from the slap. Immediately, Olivia felt bad. Kneeling down on one knee, she wiped her daughter's tears and checked to make sure her anger didn't leave any marks on Quinn's pretty face.

"I'm sorry. I didn't mean to react like that. I don't understand, what has gotten into you?" Quinn folded her arms and turned her back. "Mannequin?" Olivia looked around to make sure no one else was watching them. "Mannequin, if you want to act like a wild monkey, I can pack your bags and take you to live in the zoo. If you want to act like the daughter of a Judge and a Doctor, then I suggest you take that attitude back to the store and get a refund."

"I don't have an attitude," Quinn turned back around, "I'm speaking my mind. I don't like hanging out with that lady and her annoying son. Just like I don't like the ballet classes you put me in or the fact that you take me on all of your *boring* job trips and force me to mingle with those boring Doctors." Olivia's face nearly broke in pieces and shattered to the church ground. She'd raised a well-behaved, well-spoken, and well-mannered child. What had gotten into her?

"Where did this come from?"

"My new friend, Joanna. Daddy went to their house to talk to her dad, and I got to play with her for the first time ever. She asked why I was wearing pigtails because they were for babies, and I told her *you* put them in my hair," Quinn folded her arms as she glared. "She asked me if I liked them and I told her no. She said, "well, if you don't like them why don't you tell your mom that you don't. It's okay to speak you—" having heard enough, Olivia stood up.

"Alright, that's enough."

"No, it's not enough, and I'm not done telling you what I don't like," Quinn put a hand on her hip. "I also don't like that you and Anna's mother are best friends, and you never let us play together, but you send me to play with that black, baboon-looking kid, and-"

"Mannequin, one more word and you'll be picking your teeth up off of this church ground," Olivia threatened, irate. "I do not take you to play with Sophia's daughter because I was afraid of an influence like this," she pointed at Quinn, referencing her nasty attitude. "Sophia's daughter is a problem child and a troublemaker. She talks back, she has no respect, and she's always in and out of that little boy Bruce's house that lives up the street. *No* child of mine will associate with such nonsense."

"Well, why do you hang out with her mother?"

"Because her *mother* and I grew up together. We've been friends for a long time, and it's not her fault she can't control her children. Until she does, I will not have you anywhere near her, do you understand me?" Quinn rolled her eyes and huffed. "Do you- *understand* me?" Olivia threatened with her eyes.

"Yes," Quinn huffed under her breath.

"And don't you ever attempt to *speak your mind* to me, your father, or anyone else for that matter, unless it's positive. You are a beautiful young lady, and you need to act like it. I warned you about your character after you wiped the salon floor with the Pastor's son. This type of behavior is unacceptable. Someday, you'll be the wife of a successful businessman, or the First Lady of the United States of America. There is no need to speak your mind. You sit still and look pretty. Your beauty is powerful enough. You will go to college, you will go to grad school and you will have a good life, and good lives never come to those that speak their minds and raise hell." Olivia stared at her daughter like she meant business. Soft wisps of Olivia's warm, chestnut-colored hair swept past her ear and caressed the skin of her neck.

Her pastel skin made her beautiful full lips stand out. She had a confident, poised strut that told the world, "I'm beautiful." *And beautiful she was.* Dr. Olivia Michelle Gray looked like a movie star. Her cold, metallic gray eyes glistened brightly, rivaling the most excellently polished suit of armor. As she scolded her daughter, she blinked, the beauty of her eyes momentarily covered by the shield of her eyelashes. By the time her eyes opened again, Quinn still hadn't recovered from her intense stare. Olivia was more of an illusionist than a deceiver. Beauty was her name, and she hid behind it and fooled the world. *Everybody but Quinn.* Dr. Gray was successful, wealthy, educated, lived in a great neighborhood, traveled often, and came from a great family. But her eyes told a different story. Suffering, loneliness, longing, desire; her eyes held it all. Over the years, Quinn learned to read right through the emotions that danced in her mother's pupils like wildfire. She always wondered where it came from. Olivia had a husband that loved her, and lived a life that any woman would want- where did the pain come from? One day, however, it was as if Olivia had mentally shut down. Quinn never understood why, or how, or when, or what caused it, but she couldn't read her mother anymore. It was as if the fire in her eyes had dwindled down to smoldering ember, and she couldn't tell what emotions were soaring just beyond those walls.

"Yes ma'am," Quinn replied faintly. She didn't understand why it was so wrong to think freely and be herself. To Quinn, it didn't matter how people felt about her. Shouldn't she have a right to speak her mind? Despite what Pandora had taught her new friend, Quinn loved her mother, she loved her father, and she wanted to please them.

"I want you to have a good life. Do *you* want to have a good life?" Olivia asked. She grabbed Quinn's hands and bought her closer.

"Yes, ma'am."

"Well, the secret to a good life is to always be peaceful. Peace is the beauty of life. It is sunshine. It is the advancement of man and the triumph of truth. Promise me you'll smile and be peaceful from now on?"

"I promise," Quinn's eyes lowered. She had so many questions to ask, but she was sure none of them would bring peace to an already heightened situation, so she did as her mother requested and smiled.

"Good. Now let's go to church." Olivia held her daughter's hand and walked beside her husband.

"Steven, keep our daughter away from Sophia's little girl. She is trouble, and I don't want Mannequin going anywhere near her."

"I wouldn't say she's *trouble*," Steven chuckled, "Joanna is a ten-year-old kid. Besides, you and Soph are close friends."

"We were, but things have been different ever since she married that pig of a man. Their little boy Joseph doesn't seem at all affected, but all of the hostility and dysfunction that man has put Sophia through has rubbed off on their daughter. Just look at how our Quinn is reacting after one visit to their house. This is not healthy, and I don't want her over there again."

"I think you're a bit over the top, Liv, but alright," Steven affirmed with a head nod.

"Ta-ber-nacle Church-of-God in Chr-Christ. Because Mau-Maury isn't the only place to find your father," Quinn sounded out the church slogan just as they reached the front door. "Who's Maury?"

"Sounds like you're ready to win the church scholarship to college," an older woman peeked through the door and smiled.

"What's a scholarship?" Quinn peered up.

"It's free money reserved for pretty eyed little girls who can sound out big words, like the ones you just spelled out," the woman laughed infectiously as Quinn's parents joined in. "Good morning, I'm mother Loretta," She smiled, extending a hand.

"Good morning, God bless you," Olivia shook her hand and smiled back.

"*Mother* Loretta?" Steven raised an eyebrow, "No way are you old enough to be anyone's church mother. You must be in your twenties." Mother Loretta laughed, amused, showing her pearly white dentures.

"I'm Olivia, this is my husband Steven, and this is our daughter, Mannequin."

"Mannequin," Loretta marveled at her name. "How uniquely beautiful. It certainly fits you." Quinn looked at Mother Loretta and smiled gracefully. She'd never seen an elderly woman so pretty. Mother Loretta looked to be in her mid-sixties. She had waist-length hair the color of winter white and gunmetal gray. Her skin was a bit faded and time-worn, but she smiled like an innocent baby. There was a twinkle in her eye and a peaceful-like aura to her energy. Quinn gazed upon her like a celebrity. "Come right on in," Loretta handed them a program. "Mannequin, would you like to attend our youth study program? We have a great time there. There are lots of snacks, games, and plenty of young people your age. I can walk down with you if you'd like."

"Can I?" Quinn turned to her parents, pleading with her eyes.

"Sure, I don't see why not," Judge Steven, agreed.

"Absolutely," Olivia agreed.

"Oh great." Loretta clasped her hands together and smiled. "I'll lead you two to your seats. You're just in time to hear our beautiful choir sing."

"Liv loves choirs," Steven mentioned.

"Well, she's getting ready to hear the best," Loretta

bragged. The Grays followed Loretta through the remarkable entryway. The second their eyes made contact inside the church edifice, their mouths dropped.

"Oh my goodness," Olivia muttered, nearly breathless. The cavernous interior was well maintained and spotlessly clean. The architecture, the carved wood, chandeliers, marble carvings, ornate doors, and the fourteen Mosaics depicting the Stations of the Cross were all so magnificent; the Grays felt as if they'd taken a plane and landed in France. The Altar was made of Italian Marble. As the choir sang, the nine thousand-piped pipe organ rang out a sound so beautiful it sounded like the heavens were about to open. It was majestic and grandiose, and one of the most beautiful sights Quinn had ever seen.

"Breathtaking," Steven shook his head in awe.

"Yes, it is," Loretta nodded before pointing to an empty pew just ahead. "There's a seat available just over there to the left. Hurry now, before someone else sits there. I'll take Mannequin downstairs." Quinn's parents waved goodbye and rushed to their seats. Olivia didn't even bother to take off her coat, her matching hat, or drop her purse. She immediately started clapping and shuffling along to the sound of the church choir's song.

"Loretta, would you usher me down to the bathroom?" Doreen, a woman rushed over to them as gracefully as her seven-month pregnant belly would allow."

"Those babies are dancing on your bladder again, I see," Loretta chuckled. "Sure I'll walk you."

"Babies?" Quinn followed them back into the vestibule.

"Yes, Sister Doreen is pregnant with triplets."

"Triplets. *Three babies?"* Quinn gasped.

"Yes, three babies," Doreen, giggled infectiously as

everyone made their way down the steep staircase.

"Me and my husband have been asking God for a baby for three years, and he's finally blessed us."

"He sure has. One baby for each year you worked his nerves praying about every five minutes," Loretta laughed, "Now you're the one that'll need the prayer."

"My mother is a doctor," Quinn smiled. "She's an obstetrician too, so she delivers babies all the time. I've seen her deliver two babies at one time, but never three."

"Who is your mother?"

"Olivia Gray." The woman's eyes grew wide.

"*Dr.* Olivia Gray?" Doreen gasped.

"That's her."

"Wow, What a small world! I've heard so much about her."

"She's upstairs in service. Maybe you can say hello afterward."

"I most certainly will. And I'll tell her you sent me. What's your name?"

"I'm Mannequin, but most people just call me Quinn."

"It is so nice to meet you, Quinn."

"You too Mrs. Doreen. God bless you with your babies." Quinn smiled just as Doreen disappeared into the ladies' room.

"Good morning, children," Mother Loretta walked into the youth center with Quinn beside her. Everyone looked up. "We have a new guest today. Everyone say Good morning to Mannequin."

"Good morning, Mannequin". A room full of children looked up and waved in unison.

"*Mannequin*? Like the dolls in the Macy's window?" Pandora raised an eyebrow. "I thought your name was just Quinn."

"Hello," Quinn waved back, blushing, excited to see Pandora. "It's short for Mannequin."

"Can I still call you Quinn? I don't trust anyone who's named after plastic."

"Sure."

"Stop it, Anna," Joseph nudged her.

"Happy Sunday, scary eyed freak," Andre smiled. Quinn looked at him and frowned, as Andre appeared before her in all his grandeur. He wore a tailored black suit with a charming red tie. His strong jawline lifted with a proud, pleasant smile, and his eyes a smoldering black. He looked much different in a suit. Quinn even found Andre to be somewhat attractive. He looked charming and smart, his voice the sound of a spoiled rich boy. But the longer he mocked and insulted her, the more unattractive he became.

"Andre!" Loretta snapped her fingers at him. "Now, we will have none of that this morning, *you hear me*? You apologize right this second for your loose remark, or I'll send you upstairs to Pastor."

"Sorry," Andre replied dryly.

"Quinn, I'm so sorry. That right there is Andre; he's the Pastor and First Lady's son. He's a little jokester, he didn't mean those words."

"We've met," Quinn gave Andre a bold stare down.

"Alright, well I'll be upstairs if you need me. Your teacher is singing in the choir so as soon as they finish up, she'll be down."

"Thank you, Mother Loretta."

"Have fun," Loretta smiled, glared at Andre one last time and then disappeared out the door.

"Great. Now that that old hag is gone," Andre rolled his eyes and began teasing Quinn again.

"Should I sweep the floor with you again, tar baby?" Quinn pursed her lips together. Everyone looked up at Quinn and then turned to Andre.

"I don't know what you're talking about," An embarrassed Andre folded his arms. "Stop bringing up old stuff."

"Where are you from, Quinn?" Joseph asked. He'd seen Quinn in passing when they were little, but he'd never been face to face with her for a formal introduction until now.

"From hell," Andre muttered, causing Pandora to giggle.

"Well, why am I in church? Send me *straight* to hell," Joseph stared at Quinn in awe.

"Ditto. She is *smoking* hot," A boy named Alex mumbled, looking on. Two twin boys named Ryan and Ronald were nearly drooling at the sight of Quinn.

"Whatever, she's scary looking," Andre muttered back.

"In your dreams dude, she looks like one of my sisters Barbie dolls." Joseph wasted no more time. He quickly walked over and extended his hand. "Hi. I'm Joseph."

"Hello, Anna's brother, Joseph." Their gazes met, and Joseph nearly dropped dead. Quinn's gray eyes were too pretty for him to handle. Quinn also found herself smitten by Joseph. The boy was perfection in coffee hues; his hair and eyes were the color of dark roasted beans, but his skin was all latte. He had a shy look about him. Quinn had seen him around the neighborhood a few times, and always in his wake were the heads of little girls turning to watch him go.

"I'm Ryan," One of the twins rushed over to extend his hand for her to shake

"I'm Ronald" the other twin hurried over.

"Hi everyone," Quinn smiled sweetly.

"Are you new here?" Joseph asked as all the boys followed Quinn to an empty table. Andre rushed toward them with an attitude.

"You can't sit there. All the new people have to sit at the new member's table."

"She can sit where she wants," Pandora defended, "Why are you being so mean, church boy?"

"Yeah, *church boy*," Quinn walked over to Andre, "Why are you being so mean?" Andre looked up at Quinn and immediately forgot the next insult waiting at the tip of his tongue.

Even as a ten-year-old little girl, Quinn's beauty was breathtaking. With her golden curls, sandy skin and rosy cheeks, she was a poet's dream. At that moment, Andre locked eyes with Quinn, and his entire body became paralyzed. He couldn't think, couldn't hear, and couldn't see a thing.

"Have it your way then," he forced the words out and pushed past her to get to the front door.

"Where are you going? We're not allowed to leave," Joseph said.

"I'm going to the bathroom, *mother*," Andre insulted. He rushed outside the youth center door, high tailed it to the men's room and slammed himself against the door. What was happening to him? As far as he knew it, all girls had cooties. *Except this one.*

Chapter 2

"When the dust settles"

Tears continued streaming from Quinn's face as her childhood memories faded into the surrounding ashes of her present reality. Tabernacle Church of God in Christ used to be one of the most *beautiful* buildings in the world. State holidays and city functions were celebrated there, bringing so many people from Virginia Beach together for so many reasons. A few hours prior, fifteen hundred people gathered inside to say goodbye to Jackson. Some were there to serve the grieving family, and some were there subconsciously cheering in a collective roar that he was dead. Because Jackson was the son of a former prestigious senator, his funeral was nationally televised. What appeared to be just another day in the city of Virginia Beach, shifted into a nightmare out of the Texas Chainsaw Massacre. Guests ran through the bloodied parking lot, toppling over torn apart limbs, and children were maimed as a panicked city watched its iconic church destroyed on live TV. Quinn stepped out of her car to look around and saw so many helpless people she'd grown up with and loved. All of them were dead. Eighty-three-year old Mother Loretta lay lifeless on the ground in the same white usher uniform she was wearing the day Quinn met her; only this time it was covered in blood. Her legs were blown off and scattered a few feet away from her, and one of her arms had been hacked off and laid by her stomach, still clutching her holy bible. A few steps away were Sister Doreen's twenty-five-year-old triplet sons, well, *what was left of them*. Next to them was another man whose body was shaking. Ryan and Ronald's bodies were dismembered and mixed up like a jigsaw puzzle across the parking lot. Everywhere Quinn looked there were people with no heads, dismembered arms, legs, and shattered glass. To the left of her was a woman around eighteen-years-old with a hole in her hand and blood pouring out of it. There was a man with an injured ankle and a child with no face. Sirens rang out in the distance, and the ones who'd made it out alive were running amuck. Some were screaming; some were crying; it looked like an apocalyptic *war zone*. Through the loud shrills and sirens, Quinn could hear the distinct sound of a man choking. It was odd that she could make out such a sound in the midst of all the surrounding chaos. She hoped that maybe he was still alive and could be helped. She walked carefully through the debris of bodies and the pools of blood until she came face to face with the choking man. Her feet instantly rooted to the ground. Her eyes distended and she grabbed her mouth in shock when she saw it was Joseph. Blood poured from his head, his body twitched manically, and a chunk of his leg was missing. Clutched in his hands like two footballs were his headless twin boys.

"Joseph!" Quinn choked out an immediate cry, "Jesus, not you." Denial coursed through her veins as she knelt down beside him. "Why did you come here? You should've just stayed home." Joseph stared at Quinn through glassed over eyes. His mouth opened as if he wanted to speak, but a chunk of his throat was missing, so it was impossible. Joseph winced and grinded his teeth, struggling to remain alive as his soul debated with death.

Quinn clamped her lips to stifle a scream. She'd been at the bedsides of so many people on their way to death, *but this was different.* Quinn had been friends with Joseph for a long time. He was the first guy she'd ever crushed on and the first guy to introduce himself to her when she came to Tabernacle. In their younger days, Quinn always joked about becoming a seamstress like Joseph's mother because Sophia always made the most beautiful clothes. Joseph wanted to do anything that involved *Quinn.* He was such a hopeless romantic, and at one point in his life, he was *so* in love with Quinn. His goal was to get married and have children. Two of them. Boys are what he preferred, and maybe if he were lucky his wife would give him twins. Where many people wanted bigger houses, newer cars, and higher-paying jobs, Joseph just wanted simplicity. He despised his father and loved his baby sister. After Pandora was rescued from the Perkins home, he protected her with his life and would stand toe to toe with anyone who tried to hurt her. Joseph was such a good guy, *flaws and all.* He'd finally got his marriage on the right track and his sons were healthy and beautiful. Fatherhood looked great on him. He had so much life to live and so much love to give. Quinn stared at Joe helplessly, wondering if there was anything she could do to keep him alive. His eyes stared back as if to say, *"no, there isn't."* Joseph appeared delirious and confused. Suddenly, he began to seize into violent jerks. His hands gripped his two sons as his eyes began to roll. He was dying. It was like watching an animal shedding its skin, a physical struggle to wriggle out of this life. It was incomprehensibly horrifying, hideous and heartbreaking. In the blink of an eye, *Joseph was gone.* Quinn could hear her heart hammering in her chest as she held her breath through it all. "God, why? Why is this happening?" Tears flew out unstoppable.

"Quinn?!" A shaky familiar voice called in the distance. *Pandora.* How would she be able to breathe again after seeing her only sibling and nephews laid out on the ground, execution-style? Quinn spun around slowly, her body blocking Joseph's face while still trying to ward off the shock.

"*Quinn.* I never- I didn't touch your husband," Pandora protested softly, "I don't know what happened in college or why it's coming out ten years later, but I'm just as confused as you. I didn't do anything. It may sound crazy, but the last person I ever slept with in undergrad was Bruce. *I thought it was Bruce.* I mean, he had a helmet on, but-" Pandora's voice grew unsure, and tears filled her eyes, recalling the memory. "I texted Bruce and told him to wear it, so if it wasn't him, I didn't know. I was drunk." Pandora looked up at Quinn and felt embarrassed and broken all over again. She'd saved herself for two years after being tortured by the Perkins'. After finally trusting another man with her body again, she'd given her all to Bruce that night. Now realizing that it was Andre? Instantly, she felt sick. Quinn studied her for a few moments.

"I believe you," she finally replied, partially incoherent. As bad as it hurt, she *knew* her friend, and she *knew* her husband. Pandora's loyalty to Quinn wasn't capable of infidelity. If left with a choice to shoot herself or sleep with Quinn's husband, Pandora would be dead without hesitation. But a man struggling through a sex addiction was different. If it can bring him so desperately low enough to sleep with strippers and hookers unprotected, would Andre be capable of taking advantage of an already emotionally distraught rape victim? If it were possible that no one would ever find out, would Andre take advantage of his best friend's first love, and his first loves best friend? *Absolutely.*

"What is *happening* right now?" Pandora's eyes widened, "I don't understand. *Andre*? I'm like a sister to him. To think of me in any other way is like incest. I don't understand you either," her mind reverted back to the scene she witnessed in Quinn's office. "That woman you were just kissing, where di... what the hell is going o...," her words were cut off by a cell phone ringing behind Quinn.

Pandora quickly averted her gaze to the sound. Her face tilted to the side. She knew that "I love rock n roll," ring tone anywhere. She jokingly set Joseph's default ringtone to it after he lost to her in Rock Band a few months ago. Every time his phone rang when she was around, she'd laugh in his face.

"Someone's phone is ringing," Pandora, stated the obvious, looking a bit dazed. Her eyes surveyed the bloody pants leg and shoes of the body behind her. Although it could've been *anybody*, a sense of panic told her that it wasn't just *anybody*.

"*Mannequin*," her voice lowered, and her breathing swallowed. Fear shot through her like electricity. Quinn bit her lip in remorse, locking her eyes with Pandora's. She struggled to find the right words to say, but she couldn't. Her lips pressed together in a slight grimace just before Pandora pushed her out of the way and saw the face of her brother and his sons. She quickly jumped back and let out a blood-curdling scream.

"No!!!" She cursed and cried, pacing back and forth in disbelief. "Joe, you promised you'd stay *home*. You swore to me you wouldn't come here." She shook her head, repeatedly stepping back. Finally, she turned her back completely, denying it all. "No. No, *God*. No!" Quinn walked over to hug her, but Pandora burst into a fit of rage and shoved away. She crumbled to the ground like a cookie, taking her heart with her. Tears ripped from her eyes as she deliriously screamed until her voice grew faint and her lungs were on fire. Minutes later, she got up and walked over to her dead brother. "Joseph I'm so sorry. Babies, Auntie is so sor-" she could barely finish her sentence before guilty sobs took over again.

"Honey, it's not your fault," Quinn walked over, attempting to comfort her a second time, "You can't blame yourself, you had no idea something like this would happen. He was just at the wrong place at the wr-

"Shut up!" An angry Pandora turned red and broke away. "Please, just shut up! You don't understand, I—" She looked up at Quinn helplessly. There was no way she could tell the truth.

Quinn leaned forward and pulled Pandora close to her. Standing in the midst of ashes and death, she hugged her friend, hoping her touch would make the darkness a little lighter. Even though Quinn's husband was involved, and there were so many questions that needed answering, the love Quinn extended to Pandora was pure, unselfish, undemanding, and free. It was an indefinite embrace that said, "I love you. I'm here for you, *and I am sorry*." They both stood there cocooned within each other for what felt like an eternity.

"...I did it." The words escaped Pandora's lips.

"Anna, you didn't do anything."

Pandora stood back and looked Quinn dead in the eyes. She clutched Quinn's hands, bracing herself. "I paid to have a bomb planted in Jackson's coffin."

Quinn blinked rapidly. Removing her hands out of

Pandora's, she stepped back. "You did what?"

"Jackson killed *everyone* I loved. He took Miss Ruby; he tried to take Eden. As a defense attorney, I've met some pretty jacked up individuals, but I have never in my life met a man *that* conniving and tactful. My mind is sharper than a tack, and he even had *me* fooled. So...*I killed him,"* Pandora confessed. "But people like Jackson leave legacies behind to finish what they started. I just wanted to make sure everything connected to him was dead." Quinn closed her eyes against the confession, but it crowded into the atmosphere anyway. There had been more talk. Quinn was sure of it, but she hadn't heard anything beyond the screaming fear that filled her head.

"You blew up my church? Are you insane?" Her head tilted, "Nevermind, don't answer that!"

"I didn't think it through. I was so angry that all of this happened right under my nose, Quinn. I didn't know what to do; I just wanted to get rid of him. I told Joseph what I was considering, and he begged me not to do it. I told him I had everything under contro- "

"What did you have under control, Anna?!" Quinn fussed, stepping back to survey the disaster around them. "Please tell me?"

"I planned to make sure –"

"Make sure of *what*? That there were over fifteen hundred people in this sanctuary, and you murdered over a third of them?! There were pregnant women and children in there! You...*monster*," Quinn jerked her head back, looking at Pandora in disgust. "You just became what you destroyed."

Pandora shook her head. She didn't have a rebuttal.

"What is *wrong* with you? Quinn rushed away from her in disbelief. She couldn't look at Pandora in the face anymore.

"Quinn, please don't go," Pandora followed her.

"Stay away from me," Quinn spun around, pointing her finger toward Pandora. "Just stay away."

"No, Mannequin, wa-"

"I said stay away!"

"Quinn, please, I'm pregnant!" Quinn froze in her tracks. So much had happened in the last month, she'd forgotten Pandora was pregnant. "I am pregnant, and I was in that church too. It took me an entire lifetime to conceive. My brother was my first friend," her voice weakened. "Those are my nephews in his hands. Although I would risk myself for loyalty, I would *never* do it at the expense of my baby, my family, or my friends. I didn't *think it through*. I just wanted Jackson to die, and now everything I tried to spare is dead too. I am scared, Quinn. I need you. *I don't know what to do*." Just as Quinn opened her mouth to respond, three police cars pulled up. She knew they'd be looking to talk to her and Andre, and she didn't want to go anywhere near him at this point. She also didn't want Pandora around in case they found something suspicious that belonged to her.

"You don't deserve *any* of my help," Quinn darted. "You were one hundred percent wrong. You should be on a slow fall to hell right now. Or p*rison*." Pandora looked up at her with a face full of guilt. Quinn wanted to continue her rant, but Pandora's eyes softened her. "*But, I love you*," she sighed, almost regrettably, "and I will do my best to protect you. Come on." Quinn turned and walked toward her car, refusing to face her friend. She couldn't believe what Pandora had done. Quinn got into her driver's seat, and Pandora got in on the passenger side. Switching the gear into drive, Quinn stepped on the gas and got out of the parking lot as fast as she could. Their friendship went much deeper than words could explain. In the midst of hell, the grace and mercy shown through the love of *a true friend* would always prevail.

Chapter 3

"If you can't get rid of the skeleton in your closet,
you'd best teach it to dance"
-George Bernard Shaw

An hour later, Pandora sat in the sand on the beach peering stone-faced at the ocean. Years ago after marriage, dating, and careers took precedence over Quinn, Eden, and Pandora's friendship, they decided they needed something to solidify it. Although they grew up together, life's different directions had separated them to a degree. The one thing they all had left in common was the beach. Whenever they needed a break, they'd all go down and relax by the shore, soak up the sun, and walk the boardwalk. They went so frequently that they each decided to pool their money together to invest in their own version of a best friend charm; *a beach house.* Down through the years, it became their home away from home, and one that they shared together. When they needed a place to vent and didn't feel like going to the Olive Garden, they would go to their beach house. When they needed a vacation but didn't have time for the lengthy travel, the beach house was their temporary getaway. Miss Ruby helped them pick out the old building, and she paid a young architect from Indonesia to sculpt it into a reflection of all three of her girls. The end result was a four thousand square foot sea cottage of four bedrooms, three bathrooms, and private access to the beach. They were all passionate about beauty but in a very simple way. They were simple, but not *simplistic*. The impeccable design and unparalleled quality is what made the property a true piece of art. There was an amazing one of a kind stone fireplace with fossilized and semi-precious stones in the living room. There were seagrass limestone floors and fossil stoned walls. The kitchen where they loved to cook had all the best Meile appliances sitting atop of quartzite and black granite countertops. It spoke of pure nakedness and muteness. The big windows offered a view of the Pacific. They hadn't been to the house since Miss Ruby passed, but today the retreat was much needed. The windows were partially open, allowing in some fresh air. Quinn stood alone in the kitchen staring out of them while various emotions washed over her. Annoyance, confusion, exhaustion, regret, anger, they churned and heated until they formed a large knot in her belly. *What would possess Pandora to do such a thing?* She thought. Couldn't she have just considered smothering Jackson with a pillow? Why did she have to destroy *everything*? Quinn hadn't the slightest idea of how to move forward from this. Four hundred plus people were dead, including Joseph and his children. Twelve hundred people were injured, and her church building was no more. A simple I'm sorry might have sufficed for their friendship, but it certainly couldn't raise the dead. Pandora had really outdone her level of crazy this time. Quinn walked out into the sand to join her friend by the ocean. Happy was Pandora's usual state, but now she appeared rigid. She looked as if her spirit had sunk into a pit of nothingness and her aura had turned monochrome. She looked like a silhouette, as if she'd walked out of a photograph and left behind blackness. Quinn had never seen her like that. Even after being kidnapped, she at least had her game face on. But this was different. There was so much pain in Pandora's eyes knowing what she did to her brother and her nephews. Quinn sat next to her and watched her cry until her lungs were practically crying out for mercy. She couldn't breathe, but she couldn't stop. A tear fell from Quinn's eyes. She didn't even try to put an arm around Pandora because she knew she was inconsolable at this point. For a long time, Joseph was the only man Pandora could trust. He was the only father figure she ever knew. Growing up, her big brother was the champion, the go-getter, and the model child her father claimed to have so carefully crafted. *She* was the extra, the buddy, the second and last. Pandora always received less support and less consideration compared to the yardstick of Joseph. She was always second best and always found lacking in some vital ingredient for success. *And Joseph hated it.* His sister was the love of his life, and he always had a soft spot for her. He hated Bruce, he blamed his mother for much of Pandora's misery, and he despised his father's feministic ways. When Joseph found out Pandora had gotten married to Jackson, all kinds of red flags went off. The day he met Jackson, Jackson couldn't even look him in his eyes. Jackson looked sneaky and deceitful, and because everything in Pandora's life went downhill when her heart was involved and her defenses were down, Joseph knew she wouldn't see it. The night before the bombing at Tabernacle, Pandora paced the floor in her kitchen while P.J sat at the table staring her down like she'd lost her mind.

"Why are you pacing the floor?" P.J asked

"Because I'm angry," Pandora hissed.

"That's evident, considering your recent track record of serial murder." Pandora spun around with flared nostrils.

"Are you judging me right now?"

"Me? The biggest drug lord of the East Coast?" P.J laughed, his big belly shaking, "No. I'm not judging you. I just want to make sure you have a clear head about what you're asking me to do?"

"My head was clear when I had your men wipe out Ashley's family on Divinity Street. I knew who lived there," She scowled. "I didn't care then and I don't care now."

"You know, I did this for you because you're like family to me. But just so we're clear- you're a lunatic," P.J shook his head in disbelief. "I sell drugs, and I make money. I don't kill kids and I don't mess with old people. I'm out here doing all of this for you. Now, you want me to take out an entire *church*? You're on a whole different level of psychotic."

"Did I pay you for your opinion, or did I pay you to do a job?" Pandora bared her teeth.

"You paid me to do a job, but I want you to get out of your emotions before I say yes." Pandora raised an eyebrow, placing a hand on her hip at P.J's nerve. "Listen, you're a good girl, but you're a *dangerous* girl when you're angry. It's okay to seek revenge, but not on the innocent. Karma will come back to you."

"If that's true, wouldn't this be *Jackson's* Karma?" She sassed. "That bastard took out someone's mother, and then he tried to take out her daughter. *Twice*. He has destroyed the lives of innocent people whom I hold near and dear to my heart, and so it's time for me to destroy everything near and dear to *his* heart. Now that he's dead, everything he loves must die along with him," Pandora's eyes darted as anger boiled deep in her system like hot lava.

It churned within her, hungry for destruction. P.J looked at her for a few seconds and saw Pandora wasn't changing her mind or backing down. He made one phone call to his men, instructing them to plant the fuel-air bomb in Jackson's coffin. Getting up from his chair, he finished the glass of juice he was drinking and placed his cup in the sink.

"I don't know how I got mixed up with you," He shook his head. "It's done. You be safe. Call me if you need anything else."

"Your money will be in your account within the hour. Thank you, I will." She gave him a cold stare.

"No more killing after this," PJ warned. "You live your life and make room for your baby. You hear me?"

"Thank you for the pep talk," She digressed and walked him to the back door so he could see his way out. Pandora was so emotionally gone at this point she could've cared less about her morals. She was on a warpath, and anyone in her way would be destroyed. Just as she walked back into the kitchen, she jumped when she saw Joseph standing against the counter, his protruding eyes glaring her down.

"What in the world. Jo-"

"You had that family on Divinity street killed?" He folded his arms.

"How did you get into my house? Why don't you ever use a doorbell like everyone else?" She complained, avoiding the question.

"You know what, for some reason, I *knew* it was you. A girl from your office connected to Eden contracts HIV out of the clear blue sky. Two days later, the entire Peterson family ends up butchered and shot to death. Next thing you know, Jackson's head ends up on his mother's doorstep in another State. But you?" He walked toward her, invading her personal space, "You ended up with a broken window and a busted lip. Enough to fool the world, but not your brother."

"Okay, *great*," She clapped sarcastically, "I'm guilty. What? Are you gonna turn me in?"

"No- Anna, I'm not gonna turn you in. Where is your conscience? There were twin babies in that house and young fathers who had absolutely nothing to do with any of this."

"Joseph," She huffed, walking down her corridor. "I just had to listen to P.J.'s rant; I don't feel like listening to yours too. What's done is done and I will not allow myself to feel sorry for it."

"That's because you're angry. You've always been ruthless when you let your anger control you. But soon and very soon the dust will settle on what you've done, and you're gonna have to live with it for the rest of your life." He followed Pandora through the hallway and into the living room.

"And I will live happily ever after," She replied sarcastically.

"Whatever. I'm not letting you blow up a church. That's out of the question."

"Again, how the hell did you get into my house?" Pandora winced, "Mind your business and don't worry about what I'm doing." She sat down on the couch. Joseph stood over her and watched, awaiting her dead soul to awaken, *but it never did*. Her heart was cold as ice, and he knew there was no stopping her.

"I know you don't love very often, but think about what you've taken away. What if something happened to me or my sons- your nephews because someone was out seeking revenge on Andrea. Huh? How would you feel then?" Pandora pursed her lips, allowing his words to sink in. She would be distraught and traumatized for the rest of her life if something happened to the only family she really had. But then she'd spend the rest of her life seeking revenge on whoever did it, so, *no*. Tossing himself in the mix wasn't going to soften her heart. Grabbing her remote, Pandora flicked on the television and traced through the channels. Anything to seem busy so Joseph would leave.

"Joanna?" Joseph's nostrils flared through his angry red face. "Answer me when I'm talking to you...Joa-"

"What!" Pandora finally roared, jumping up from the chair. "I'm angry, okay? Jackson is going to pay." Her voice weakened and tears filled her eyes. Joseph always did have the power to get a rise out of her.

"He paid, baby," Joseph grabbed her arms and pulled his sister into an embrace. "He's dead. He didn't win. Killing his extended family isn't going to bring back Miss Ruby. It won't change the fact that you let your heart lead you in the wrong direction, and it won't take away the suffering that Eden went through." Pandora cried, hanging on to her brother. She was so furious; she didn't know *what* to do other than keep on killing until the feeling passed. She blamed herself for allowing her heart to fail her a second time. After Bruce, Pandora promised herself she would never fall in love again. Strong women didn't fall in love anyway; they treaded in love. They flirted with it. They embodied it with caution and then they escaped from it unscathed. She told herself the day she walked into Jackson that he'd just be a rebound. He would serve as a fling, a friend with benefits, or maybe even a domestic partner, but never, *ever* would he become her lover. At the end of loving Bruce, Pandora felt crippled and small. She was criticized when she loved hard and criticized when she didn't love hard enough. Detachment was her new goal. She told herself she wouldn't feel a *thing*. But somewhere along the lines, things became blurry, and she ended up a wife and almost lost a friend. People were dead and lives were destroyed *because of her,* and she was *angry.* Blowing up a church full of Jackson's family wouldn't even be enough to calm her storm. She would have had to make a deal with the devil to become the anti-Christ and all of humanity would need to be destroyed for her to feel like she'd won. Rubbing her back, Joseph held her tightly. "You have a baby in your belly. You're a walking miracle. Babies are proof that life must go on. They're gifts from God. God loves you. *He's given you mercy,* and you want to blow up his *church*? Come on, Anna. Simmer down and think with your head, not your broken heart. Your heart is what got you into this mess." Joseph was right. Maybe Pandora should've called everything off. *No.* Her head and her heart were in full sync of the destruction that was to come. *There was no more time for thinking. The damage had already been done.*

....

Pandora stared out into the ocean as the sound of the waves washed away her memory. *If only she'd listened to P.J. or Joseph.* They were right. Pandora had given Jackson *his* Karma, and the Karma she dished out had come right back to *her.* If only she could go back in time.

"I wish you'd have thought this through before you made such a rash decision," Quinn finally spoke, "but just like everything else we've conquered in life, we'll get through this one. I have your back. We'll see to it that no one ever finds out what happened. I love you, okay?" And love, Quinn certainly did. Friendship is a form of love, and Quinn was a woman who always loved in full measure. She took the good times and fought through the bad. She was there for every heartbreak, she helped to ease every pain, and she saw Pandora for the human being she was. Throughout the storms of her friend's lives, she didn't just climb in the boat with them; *she became the boat*. All true love requires a sacrifice of the self to be real. It was more than words. *It required action*. The love that poured through their friendship was accepting, compassionate, unconditional, without judgment, and eternal. It forgave and endured, and today was just another day to prove it.

"I love you, too," Pandora's voice shook as she wiped away the continuous stream of tears from her eyes. "You are the epitome of *everything* I wish I would've become."

"Me?" Quinn tilted her head.

"Yeah, you," Pandora nodded. "With almost everything, you keep your challenges to yourself. Even from Eden and I at times. You're like this beautiful mystery that I never could figure out. As soon as I think I've got you down pat, you shift into another cocoon."

They both shared a much-needed giggle before Pandora placed her hands into Quinn's.

"I know this has got to *hurt*. Your husband, your church, but you never deal with anyone or anything from a place of pain, and I'm so grateful to be your friend. At first glance, many people think you're quiet and shy. Shy, you're not. Quiet, I've never been too sure. My experience is that you've always chosen your words very carefully. You are observant and wise beyond your years. Shoot, your wisdom has certainly saved me many more times than I want to admit. Like now."

"I think you give me way too much credit," tears glazed down Quinn's eyes as she laughed out loud. I'm not

as grounded and centered as you think I am. If anyone is a master at being a leader, it's you. Many times in your presence, I feel like you're the master and I'm the student."
Pandora lifted an eyebrow.

"Girl please, all I am is a ticking time bomb."

"*You* see a time bomb. I see brute honesty and an absolute shut off valve. When you're done, *you're done*. You have a strength about you that I've never seen in another woman. You are *bold*. Where many people leave periods, you leave exclamation marks."

"I disagree," Pandora retorted.

"Honey, you just blew up my megachurch," Quinn gave her an incredulous stare. Pandora turned away, embarrassed, allowing Quinn to finish. "You have very few friends, but you have this fierce loyalty to Eden and I that is deeper than anything I can ever try to explain. You lack the guile and complexity of my other friends; what you see is what you get. You are refreshing, and you are for life. You aren't simply just a *good friend;* you've become part of my soul. I love you like a sister. There's this kindred spirit between us and I couldn't abandon you any more than I could my own daughter."

"Well, I hope you mean that, because you and Eden, and Bruce," she rubbed her belly, "and this little miracle is all I have left. *I don't have my big brother anymore.* My mind can't even comprehend how to push forward. It feels like my entire childhood just vanished. Joseph and I were so close and effortless friends, and now just like that, because of me, he's gone. I'll never forgive myself for this. With anyone else, I'm a lioness, but with Joseph, I was a rabbit. One look from him and the fight just would leave my body. He saw me for who I was inside. He quelled that inferno. Whenever he was around, my soul was at rest and content, and I just-" her breath caught as Pandora became at a loss for words and started to cry again. Quinn stood up and opened her arms. Standing up, Pandora stepped into Quinn's embrace and hung on like she was never going to let go. *Everyone was going to miss Joseph.*

"There you guys are," Eden rushed out the back door and scurried over to them.

"Hey," Quinn said, as she and Pandora turned in unison, trying to fix their flustered faces.

"All of Virginia Beach is going to hell, and y'all are at the beach house having coffee," she folded her arms, "What the heck?"

"I'm sorry. I needed to get away for a moment to try and process things," Quinn rubbed her temples.

"Process what?" Eden's head tilted. "The bomb in Jackson's casket, Andre and Bruce fighting like two angry bulls, or you kissing that woman back there?" A long silence filled the beach. It was almost like the waves were even waiting for an answer. Finally, Eden asked, "are you bisex—"

"No," Quinn quickly cut her off. "I'm not bi-sexual-I'm not a lesbian. I'm not attracted to women."

"Well, her tongue was in your mouth, and everyone saw it, including your husband and he is on fi-"

"I don't care *what* you saw and I don't care how fired up Andre is about it!" Quinn snapped, pointing a finger in Eden's direction. Surprised, Eden stepped back, and Pandora stared widely. Neither of them had ever experienced Quinn's temper.

"I'm sorry," Eden swallowed.

"Wait, no." Quinn took a deep breath and got herself together. Immediately, she felt guilty. "*I'm sorry.* I didn't mean to scream."

"Quinn, what's going on? Clearly, we know what we saw," Pandora chimed in.

"I know," Quinn lowered her head, embarrassed. "Look, it's a long story to tell, okay?"

"Well, I reckon if you'd been honest with the people closest to you, there wouldn't be a long a story to tell," Pandora crossed her arms.

"That's not fair," Quinn winced at Pandora, "Don't throw stones at *me*, glasshouse. Weren't you messing around with *Bruce*?" her eyebrows lifted. "Doesn't the baby in your belly prove that you're *still* messing around with Bruce?"

"Baby?" Eden's eyes crowded with genuine confusion, "What baby?"

"Well gee, thanks a lot Quinn," Pandora flung her hand in the air. "That's not how I wanted people to find out."

"Oh my Goodness, Anna, you're having a *baby*?" Eden's face lit up.

"I am having a baby," Pandora confirmed with a warm smile.

"*Bruce's* baby?"

"Bruce's baby," she blushed. Eden screamed cheerfully, rushing over to Pandora with the happiest hug. She kissed her cheeks over and over again before rubbing her belly and screaming some more. Eden was so happy for her friend. She'd been rooting for her and Bruce for years and was so elated to learn they'd found their way back to one another. "I'm so happy for you," tears welled up in Eden's eyes.

"Thank you; I'm excited too."

"Quinn and I are Godparents, right?"

"Absolutely," Pandora released her hug. "Well, as

soon as Quinn stops dodging our question about liking women," she joked. Quinn's eyes flashed with immediate anger. She looked like lightning on a pitch-black night.

"I *do not* like women."

"*I beg to differ*," Diamond smirked, gracing the beachfront with her presence as she walked over to them. All three girls looked up.

"Oh no, are you serious? Why are you here?" Quinn looked annoyed.

"Who the heck are you and why are you in our yard?" Eden jerked her head back.

"This is Quinn's property too, correct? She invited me here multiple times during our rendezvous." Eden and Pandora looked at Quinn. Their faces dropped like dead bodies.

"Whatever, don't lie on me," Quinn's face turned red. Eden and Pandora jerked their heads in shock. They'd never heard Quinn use that kind of tone before.

"*Okay*," Diamond laughed, "So maybe we didn't get past second base, but you know you wanted to. I'm also certain we would have if you'd have listened to me." Every time Diamond talked, Quinn got angrier. "I told you your husband was nothing but a lying, scandalous, cheat. I even proved it to you after I pocket dialed you while I slept with him. *In your house.* He's a liar and everyone knows it." Quinn's eyes were a knife in Diamond's ribs, the sharp point digging deeper. Her unmoving gaze was accompanied by deliberate slow breathing as if she were fighting something back. *And loosing.* "Cat got your tongue?" Diamond mocked.

"I told you not to do that," Quinn spoke slowly, controlling her temper. "I don't care what you think about me, and I don't care what point you tried to make. I am not leaving my husband, and I certainly wouldn't leave him for a woman- a manipulator at that."

"Manipulator?" Diamond winced through a devious grin, "Are you referring to me, or you?" She looked over at Pandora. "Hi, Anna, it's nice to see you again after all these years."

"Do I know you?" Pandora furrowed.

"Not really. I saw you in passing a few times at my grandfather's house. You *were* locked in his basement, correct?" Pandora snapped her neck up at Diamond. "I spent many nights in his bedroom when my parents dropped me off before they went to work. You're not the only one he violated. I'm shocked Quinn didn't tell you." Diamond smirked, shifting her gaze toward Quinn, "yet, *I'm* the manipulator?" Pandora opened her mouth to speak, but she'd forgotten how to breathe. She looked over at Quinn for answers, but the Quinn she'd known wasn't there anymore. Quinn's eyes narrowed at the woman who continued to taunt her. The way her eyes squinted and glared reminded Pandora of a pit viper's slit-like pupils. *Something caged was about to come out and play.*

"Diamond, you need to leave before you do any more damage," Quinn demanded.

"I'm not going anywhere. You hurt me! I trusted you, I confided in you, and I cared about you. How could you embarrass me this way?"

"Dear God, embarrass you *like what?* You caught me at a vulnerable moment when my marriage was a train wreck. We kissed and it was a mistake," Quinn looked at Diamond like she could throw up. "I'm married; I have a child. You are *sick*. Have you lost your mind?"

"Apparently I have, thinking we were something we weren't," Diamond walked up to Quinn. "I should've known you were just using me for your own benefit. You appeared so nice and sweet when I walked into your office. I thought we'd become good friends," Diamond shook her head slowly, "but considering you knew your *best* friend was stuck in a dungeon the entire time, and you left her there to rot for nine months before you actually did something to help her, I should've known you were disloyal." Pandora gasped in horror, blankly staring at Quinn.

"What?" Eden looked at Quinn, confused and angry. "Quinn, what's she talking about?" Quinn looked rigid, cold, and hard. Every word Diamond spoke was like gasoline to the fire burning inside of her. Her fists began to clench, and her jaw rooted.

"Oh," Diamond playfully put a hand over her lips, "That's right, you never told her about the deal your-"

"Shut *up!*" Quinn exploded. Burning rage hissed through her body like a deadly poison. With one hand, she reached for Diamond's neck. Her anger was so powerful; it looked like she was causing objects to levitate. Effortlessly, she lifted Diamond off her feet. Pandora and Eden looked on in fear. They both backed away as their primal instinct took over. Quinn gripped Diamond's neck like a python and started to choke the life out of her. Diamond's face was white as chalk. Her eyes and mouth were frozen wide open in an expression of stunned surprise. One year ago, Diamond, formerly known as Desiree Pitts, walked into Quinn's office seeking help to get through a nasty divorce. Her ex-husband, pastor James Pitts had cheated on her with multiple women in their church and then divorced her. Diamond left the state of Arizona where her home and church were and flew back to her birthplace of Virginia Beach, in search of freedom. She couldn't find much without any money or collegiate degree to secure a good job. What she did find, was a strip club. Diamond used her beautiful body to afford herself a decent living. It was either that or a homeless shelter, so she chose to strip. But that wasn't who she was. It wasn't how she was raised and eventually she became depressed, degraded, and lost. She searched the yellow pages for a therapist and discovered Dr. Mannequin Bentley. On the day of her appointment, she crawled into Quinn's office begging to be set free. Quinn invited her to church and helped her as best as she could during their counseling sessions. She taught Diamond that all emotional pain had a biological purpose to teach and to educate us away from unhealthy patterns and relationships. *Maybe Quinn should've taken her own advice.* In her own unhealthy marriage, Quinn had been pushing back against pain for so long. She medicated herself through friendships and false romantic notions, yet her reality returned in her weaker moments and devastated her mind. Quinn blacked out and squeezed Diamond's neck tighter and tighter for everything that had *ever* happened to her. *Everything she held in.* She squeezed for her dead mother and her unfaithful husband. She squeezed for the miscarriage she had in college after a car accident, and she squeezed for Joseph's wife making a mockery of her marriage. She squeezed for the death of Joseph and his infant children, and she squeezed for Eden and Miss Ruby. At one point, Quinn knew she needed to let Diamond go, but something in her refused. Many people weave in and out of sanity and insanity, completely unaware that they've crossed over. For some, insanity is just a toe in the water, testing it out, and then they return home. But for others, it is possible to venture out too far to where you're unable to find your way back home. With a final squeeze, Diamond fell limp into Quinn's grasp. Letting her go, her body slumped into the sand. One minute Diamond was right in Quinn's face, more alive than she had ever been. The next, she was meat on the floor. *Dead.* Quinn's bags had long been packed, the house of sane had been collecting dust. A long time ago she hopped on a one-way trip to insanity with no money to buy a ticket home. Her degreed education, her Pastor's wife façade and her beauty did her justice. Her humble, meek spirit had everyone fooled, *but not anymore.* Quinn looked at Diamond's lifeless body and didn't feel the least bit bothered by it. Her eyes lifted to meet her friends, and they were both stunned. Pandora and Eden's lips were parted and their eyes were as wide as they could stretch. And there stood Quinn. Bare. Naked. Exposed, with the gentle water wading behind her. There was a reason Quinn loved the Ocean so much. It was gentle, soft, and clean, but it was also powerful and contained enough force to destroy everything. But then, *the most innocent faces were the wildest.*

Chapter 4

Three years ago...

It was a bright summer day in the city of Virginia Beach, Virginia. Quinn and Pandora sat on the Porch of Pandora's mother's house, watching Sophia as she gardened. It was Sophia's birthday, and while Pandora hated coming home and would always give a million excuses as to why her schedule wouldn't permit it, Quinn had a way of making her feel terrible about it, so she always went. Big Joseph had gotten laid off years ago and was out golfing with Joseph and some of his friends. Pandora was relieved because the sight of her father always made her sick to her stomach.

"The weather broke early this year," Sophia declared.

"It did," Quinn confirmed. "Your roses look beautiful."

"Brenda's are much nicer. I wish mine looked like hers, but I'm content with how these came out." Quinn watched Pandora look in another direction and roll her eyes. Sophia had a beautiful garden full of lush bushes and blooming flowers that were artfully arranged and professionally displayed, yet, Sophia couldn't see it. She could never take a compliment without giving glory to someone else. Pandora hated that her mother had so much potential but refused to utilize it. She never gave herself enough credit for anything. Whatever Big Joseph told her she was, she was. Every time Pandora returned home it was like stepping back into the fifties. Quinn's kind heart and ability to see things from other people's perspectives challenged her friend to respect her mother's frugal nature. Sophia was married to a controlling husband who had been recently laid off and was now broke. As a result, Sophia had lived the last five years squeezing every penny until it was reduced to base elements.

"Thank you, girls, for my wonderful tennis bracelet," Sophia said. "I really wish y'all wouldn't have spent so much money. You should've put it into a savings account for a rainy day." Quinn went to answer, but an annoyed Pandora responded first

"A simple thank you without all the *"you didn't have to spend the money"* talk, would suffice. We just wanted to do something nice for you. You deserve it." Sophia was already shaking her head.

"Have I taught you nothing? Nice doesn't have to cost three thousand dollars. A simple card would've meant so much more."

"Oh, for the love of-" Quinn cut Pandora off with a soft nudge to the side.

"I'm not like you, Anna, I don't believe in that sort of thing."

"Liking nice things?"

"No, wasting money the way you do. You're never content with what you have. You always have to have more."

"Like those red shoes?" Quinn began to laugh as Sophia shook her head at her daughter. Pandora and Quinn were thirteen years old when they spotted a pair of red, patent leather shoes in a department store while out Christmas shopping with their parents. They were the most beautiful shoes either of them had ever seen in their lives, and they wanted them. Quinn's mother purchased them for her daughter without hesitation. Pandora's mother told her no.

"You already have your school shoes and your play shoes. If you need something fancy, which is unlikely for a thirteen-year-old, you can borrow the pair Mannequin has."

Pandora was so disappointed. She wanted those shoes with fiery desperation and did everything she could to get them. She'd tried begging, bargaining, and even attempted to sell some of her old electronics to neighborhood kids, but no one wanted her modest hand me downs. Christmas morning had come and gone, and Pandora had gotten three presents. None of them were her red shoes. Years later she started babysitting. Eventually, she saved enough of her own money and purchased a pair of ridiculous high-heeled patent leather pumps. Sophia was horrified. Pandora was supposed to be saving for her future, but she told her mother she'd been dreaming about red patent leather shoes for six years and was past due. It wasn't until later that Pandora realized the pumps she'd bought were more suitable for someone who dabbled in prostitution than a high school sophomore. Quinn and Eden laughed at Pandora so much that she'd only worn them a few times, but they'd represented something significant: she'd wanted them, and she had bought them herself. Buying those shoes represented possibilities and freedom. Pandora decided then and there she was going to make enough money to buy whatever she wanted, whenever she wanted. No one was ever going to tell her no again.

"Laugh all you want. I was determined to get what I wanted, and that'll never change."

"Until you end up bankrupt like your father,"

Sophia shook her head.

"You *do* know I have a savings account, right?" Pandora asked her mother. "And a 401K."

"I hope it's enough."

"Mom, I'm the CEO of a billion-dollar law firm. I know how to handle money." Sophia glanced around as if concerned someone would overhear them.

"Keep your voice down. There's no reason to go bragging to the whole neighborhood. That sort of thing is private."

"Right. Because aside from not spending money, you don't like to talk about it either," Pandora huffed.

Big Joe used to be a millionaire, but after being frivolous with his money and then getting laid off, Pandora had no idea what he made now. Whatever it was, she was sure Sophia only saw the chump change from it. Sophia had no idea what Pandora made either. She had a feeling her mother would faint with shock at her mid-six-figure salary.

"I'll be right back. Let me run and plug the hose in." Sophia walked to the other side of the yard as Pandora watched in disappointment. For the four hundred millionth time, she wished her mother were different. An impossible request, of course, but she couldn't shake the feeling of sadness when she thought of Sophia. She had so much to offer, yet chose to live such a small life with an abusive husband. Pandora's love of exotic destinations and fancy jewelry came from the times she and her mother would check out travel books from the library. They would ogle the colorful pictures and talk about going there...*someday*. Pandora eventually learned that for her mother, "someday" really meant never. Once she'd broken free and bought her red shoes, she'd also decided she was going to see the world. And she had. She supposed for Sophia, her garden was enough.

"Anna, please don't act like this. It's her birthday," Quinn looked at Pandora with pleading eyes.

"Why did I even subject myself to coming here just to listen to her rant about me being a disappointment? *I didn't follow the family rules, I'm not modest, or average enough. I'm too driven and too flashy.*"

"I'm sure she means well."

"She knows about my new beachfront condo, but she's never seen it. No doubt her senior heart would give away if she did," Pandora chuckled.

"Your mother loves you. Love comes in many forms," Quinn's eyes watered. "Be grateful you have a mother who is alive and loves you. You and Sophia have your differences, but if something bad were to happen she'd be right there for you."

Pandora looked up at Quinn and felt bad. It was evident that Quinn still missed her own mother. If Pandora couldn't get it together for herself, she could at least do it for Quinn.

"You know what, you're right. We'll only be here a few more hours. The least I can do is be gracious."

"Thank you," Quinn smiled, relieved.

"You know Jackson brought up having children one day," Pandora changed the subject.

"Did he?" Quinn looked surprised.

"Yeah, and it'll never happen. I'm too busy. I'm thirty-five now. Maybe when I'm thirty-nine or forty we can try."

Sophia walked up with raised eyebrows and her mouth twisted with judgment.

"Anna. No. You can't. You'd be too old."

An unexpected slap, Pandora thought.

"Forty is not old," Pandora defended.

"You'd be close to sixty when your child graduated from high school. Are you sure you could even get pregnant at that age? Besides, I don't even see you getting married. *Ever.* Are you even dating?" Sophia's eyes widened. "You're not gonna try to adopt a foreign child, are you?" Quinn turned her head to keep from laughing.

"I might." Because the stubborn kid in Pandora thought defying her mother sounded pretty darned good right about now.

"I have no idea what your father would say about that." Pandora wanted to find her way to the golf course and tell him that second. *In front of his friends.* Instead, she drew a breath and let the urge wash over her. Getting up, she grabbed her glass.

"I'm going to get more juice," she said with an attitude before hurrying away.

Sophia looked at Quinn who tried so hard to get her snickers under control.

"I know she hates me."

"Who could ever hate you?" Quinn replied, amused.

"I'm serious. We don't see eye to eye at all. Maybe if she wasn't so evil..."

"I wouldn't say she's *evil.* More like she knows who she is and what she wants out of life. I admire her rigid exterior as a woman. Not everyone has guts like her," Quinn chuckled.

"Call it what you want, that child is evil," Sophia pursed with a laugh, "She came out of the womb with a nasty attitude. When she was about six months old, she was determined to walk, but her legs weren't strong enough so she would roll everywhere."

"That sounds like Anna," Quinn shook her head.

"But you. You were always so different, Mannequin." Putting her gardening tools away, Sophia sat down beside Quinn. "I don't see how you two managed as friends all these years. With her attitude and your meekness, it's like the angelic and the demonic joining forces."

"Miss Sophia," Quinn winced, "You're criticizing your only daughter. *Did you forget who raised her?*"

"I didn't raise her. She didn't want me as a mother. I was never good enough for her and she blamed me for her kidnapping."

"That's not true. I think you're being a bit-"

"Mannequin," her demeanor shifted, and her voice elevated. "Joanna wanted nothing to do with me after she was rescued and you *know* it. She ran to Ruby and let *Ruby* raise her. *Ruby* paid for her prom, saw her through college, and paid for her to go to law school. I took no part in her success, so I could care less that she's amounted into some hotshot lawyer. *My* little girl wanted to be a nurse. *Ruby's* little girl wanted to be a lawyer. "*Miss Ruby,*" her lips curled. "That woman made a mockery of my mothering skills throughout this town. And she called herself *holy,* and a woman of God. May her soul rest-in-*peace,*" Sophia's voice was laced with bitterness. It's a good thing they buried her with her church fan. I'm sure she needs it where she is." Quinn shook her head. She wanted to revert to First Lady mode and tell Sophia that operating in the spirit of bitterness opened the door for every demon in hell to have legal access over her life. There a reason everyone in Sophia's life had moved on to bigger and better things while she still remained the same; abused, battered, regretful, resentful, and *bitter*. If she didn't learn to let the past go and allow God to heal her broken heart, she would forever be a tormented soul. However, per Olivia's request for Quinn never to speak her mind unless it was something positive, she digressed and continued to listen. After ending her rant, Sophia looked at Quinn and just stared as if she were reminiscing.

"What's the matter?"

"Nothing really. You just remind me so much of your mother, is all," Sophia smiled.

"I get that a lot," Quinn replied.

"And it's nothing short of the truth. You are your mother's child. I sure do miss my friend. I took her tragic death harder than I did when my own parents died. We were tied at the hip since grade school. We graduated together, we got married around the same time, and we were pregnant with our girls together. It's funny because Liv told me she'd never have children, but when we got to Virginia State, and she met your father, all of that changed."

"Oh really?" Quinn's smile instantly faded.

"Yeah," Sophia smiled, unaware of Quinn's shift in demeanor.

"Her and your daddy were so in love. Just before she went off to medical school, I met my own husband, and he kept me company while Liv was away. *Too much company*, because I ended up pregnant a second time. Olivia and I would talk on the phone every day and write each other once a month, but I was too ashamed to tell her I was pregnant a second time. Liv and I had such big dreams. She was out living hers, and I was a housewife, pregnant again. One day, Liv came home from school for a visit. I'll never forget, she knocked on my door, and when I realized it was her, I was too ashamed to open it because I wasn't ready to tell her I had gotten pregnant. "

"So what happened?"

"I pretended like I wasn't home, but it was pointless because she had a key. She barged in and chased me all up and through my house before I finally gave in and turned around to face her with a face full of tears. To my surprise, her belly was just as big and pregnant as mine." Tears fell from Sophia's face. "We both just stood there like two pregnant fish, embarrassed, but relieved we could go through it together. I never could imagine life without her by my side, and although she's not here anymore, I see what we had manifesting through you and Anna. Minus the pregnancy of course. I don't think my Anna will ever have children."

"I'm glad to have her and Eden as friends. Life is much more bearable with them around," Quinn smiled.

"Yeah. I always said that if Livi were still here, Anna would've never gone to live with Ruby. Olivia *loved* Anna. She was the greatest mother in the world, and she raised you with dignity and class. I modeled her skills. She had that nurturing warmth about her, coupled with her Doctor's expertise. She would have shown me how to be there for my baby the way I needed to be."

"You guys were friends for so long. Decades, I've heard. I wonder why Anna and I never got to play together until Middle School," Quinn implied. She already knew the answer, but she always wondered if Sophia knew.

"Well, you know you were always sick as a child," Sophia replied with a somber glow. Quinn raised an eyebrow and parted her lips. *Sick?* "Apparently, vaccinations didn't work for you. Olivia didn't want your ailments being passed on to Anna, so she kept you away." *What a fruit loop*, Quinn thought, batting her pretty eyes at

Sophia. Olivia Gray was the best doctor in the country. Quinn could count on her fingers the number of times she had so much as a sore throat growing up. Quinn was suddenly glad that things happened in Pandora's life in the way that they did. While unfortunate, they separated her from an abusive father and a weak-minded, do-do brain of a mother. Pandora would have *never* become who she was if Sophia and Big Joe had continued raising her. *God had a plan all along.* Olivia was the only friend Sophia had, and would probably ever have. Down through the years, she protected Sophia and did everything she could to save her from Big Joe's wrath. Olivia also did everything she could to keep Sophia and Joseph's problem child of a daughter away from Quinn. Her lies about Quinn being sick apparently worked until Middle School. Considering there was only one grade school in Virginia Beach, the two girls eventually became close friends in sixth grade. Olivia was upset, but at that point, there was nothing she could do anymore.

"Do you ever still talk to your father?" Sophia changed the subject.

"I'm sorry?" Quinn gave her an incredulous stare.

"Your father. Judge Gray."

"Um, no. I haven't," Quinn replied. After it was discovered that Judge Steven wasn't Quinn's real father, he walked away from Quinn and her mother and has never spoken another word to them. Word of it had gotten around to close friends and family, but it was never made public. Eventually, it became a hidden secret that was buried with Olivia Gray to keep her superb character intact.

"You know, I still find it a shame that that drug dealer from back in the day would frame your mother like that."

"Maybe we should just change the subject." Quinn felt herself becoming flustered and upset.

"No. We shouldn't. I know it's a sore spot for you, Mannequin, but you need to hear the truth. That man, Josiah, he dated your mother during freshman year of college. They both thought they were in love and talked about getting married. Then, he got into drugs, so Livi dumped him and he went crazy. He tried to get her back, but she'd moved on to your father. Your father became a Judge, and Olivia became a Doctor. Josiah was jealous and tried everything he could to frame your mother and ruin her life. He paid to have blood samples switched and everything. It was a deceitful mess, and Steven believed it. You need to go talk to him and set the record straight," Sophia darted her eyes and pointed at Quinn. "Steven didn't even show up to Livi's funeral. You two need each other. Please stop this madness."

"Well, thank you," Quinn stood up quickly, brushing the dust off the back of her pants. "I think I'm gonna go have some of whatever juice Anna is drinking." Quinn turned to walk away.

"Mannequin," Sophia called. Quinn rolled her eyes before turning back around. "Did you hear everything I said?"

"I heard you," Quinn politely smiled at her *deceptive behind*. After twelve years as a psychologist, she was still amazed at people's ability to lie with a straight face.

Chapter 5

"One's life is sacred. It is lived as a secret, and told as a lie"

Six months had passed since the bombing of Tabernacle Church of God in Christ. There had been no leads, no fingerprints, or valuable information to help police figure out who was responsible. As an accountant, Jackson built his financial empire through manipulation, schemes, and finding crafty ways to steal from his clients in ways he thought they'd never realize. Over fifty of them began coming forward with allegations just before his death, so it was possible that any of them could've been responsible. Jackson also had relatives who dibbled and dabbled in illegal activity throughout the years, so the bomb could've been a personal attack to get rid of his entire family in one shot. There were so many possibilities, but no evidence, which meant *no one could ever be charged.* Thankfully, Andre's parents had good insurance on their church, and it was more than enough to have a brand new one built. In the meantime, what was left of the Tabernacle's members began to meet in hotel conference rooms for Sunday morning services and bible studies. The gunshot wound Andre suffered at the hands of Pandora had nearly taken his arm off. The bullet entered his flesh and then broke into pieces, causing him to suffer through a grueling sixteen-hour surgery to remove the fragments, thus saving his arm. And he suffered through the surgery *alone.*

One month after the church bombing, Quinn and Andre's marriage took a turn for the unfortunate worse; the kind of worse *nobody* would ever see coming. Since middle school, they had been inseparable. Each was the center of the universe for the other. They were inevitable, caring, and relaxed in each other's company throughout the years. Despite flaws, death, tragedy, and even addiction, Quinn and Andre remained devoted to one another with a promise never to stray. *But some things were unforgivable.* Rape was one of them. Infidelity with the same sex was another. Quinn couldn't stand to even look at Andre knowing what he'd done to Pandora. Her once soft eyes toward him turned cold, as did the temper Andre never knew she had. Words flew from her mouth that he never thought she'd think, let alone say out loud. Andre knew instantly from the look in Quinn's eyes that their marriage had hit their mark. *And the feeling was mutual.* Quinn was the love of Andre's life, and he prided himself in the satisfaction that she'd never been with anyone else. *Or so he thought.* Not only had she been with someone else, she'd been with a *woman.* How was he supposed to compete with that? Weeks of frustration, rebellion, arguing, and screaming filled their home.

"Mannequin, I need you to come to church with me. The congregation needs you; the women need you, and they've been asking about you. I can't keep up this lie about you being sick much longer," Andre fussed, walking into Quinn's personal space.

"You've been keeping up a lie for the last twenty years, why is it a problem now?" she leaned closer, perfectly composed.

"People in glass houses shouldn't throw stones," his face mottled crimson as his eyes popped and his tree-trunk neck strained.

"Then put *your* stones down and retreat back into your *glasshouse*," Quinn remained as still as a cadaver and just as pallid, unblinking against his onslaught. Then, with a barely concealed smirk, she turned on her heels and walked away as if strolling in the park on a fine day. Andre's temper simmered and fizzed like a firework.

"Excuse me!?" He followed her, "I have been upfront and honest with you about my demons. I cheated on you *once* since we've been married!" Quinn spun around.

"You told me you had a sex addiction, you didn't mention you were a rapist," she hissed. "Just how many women in the church *have* you slept with?"

"Me? How many women in the church have *you* slept with?" Andre's booming voice shook the walls as his words spewed out with the ferocity of a machine gun.

Quinn's eyes popped open. *If looks could kill.* "That's right, I said it. I'm not the only lying, scandalous cheat in this house!" Andre's temper was like TNT, once the sparks started to sizzle there was very little time to duck and cover. Quinn knew she should've just stayed quiet, but she couldn't help sparring with him. Like trained boxers, they circled one another. The gloves were off. It was fighting time.

"You are an insult to the body of Christ!" Quinn exploded with unrestrained fury.

"Whatever you say, Jezebel."

"I should have listened to my father. He *told* me to be careful with you years ago!"

"Father?" Andre jerked his head back, "Which one? The crack head, or the Judge? I don't remember."

They traded slur for slur, insult for insult, dig for dig until their relationship shattered into glassy shards.

Nothing would ever be the same again, and both of them knew it. Their love had turned to poison. Finally, they made a mutual decision to separate. Quinn moved out and into a condo and Andre moved into an apartment. They put their house up for sale and shared equal responsibility for Heaven. Andre kept her Monday through Wednesday, and Quinn kept her Thursday to Sunday. It was hard watching the family Quinn always wanted crumble before her very eyes. Over the months, Quinn grew depressed and her days became cold and empty with the realization that she would never be happy again. Pandora had gotten rid of Diamond's body as an IOU, but even she hadn't spoken another word to Quinn since. Quinn couldn't bear to look her best friend in the face anymore anyway knowing everything Diamond exposed about her, so their feelings were mutual. She knew she had a lot of explaining to do, but Pandora was too pregnant, and too much of a hormonal hothead to be willing to listen to anything she had to say so Quinn kept her distance. Eden didn't understand what was going on, but she saw sides of Quinn that made her fear for her life, so she stayed away and kept things cordial as well. A text here and there. An email every so often. Quinn lost her friends, her church, and her husband. All she had left was three days of motherhood. She drank too much wine, didn't eat enough food and had long given up ever feeling normal again. She knew down to the minute how long ago her life did a complete 360. She resented Andre, and she yearned for him in equal measures. Quinn was lost and alone and yet, had apparently learned to fake it so well, no one bothered to ask her how she was doing. She protected her pain from outside scrutiny as she'd always done. She went to work everyday and smiled through the pain. As a psychologist, she committed all of her strengths, might, and ability into creatively helping others, but sadly failed to apply the same profound sayings, methods, applications and notions in her own life challenging situations. A majority of Psychologists have bad marriages and relationships, and it's almost impossible to save. Teaching is easy, and preaching is powerful, but practicing what we preach is *hard work*. Quinn knew as a therapist she'd be tempted with the same problems she solved for others. Her advice to them was to first acknowledge the problem and then seek out help. Finally, she decided it was time she took her own advice.

"You and Pandora seem to have a close-knit friendship," her therapist, Dr. Gwenn Baker confirmed, "I wonder if she still has those shoes."

"She does, actually," Quinn managed a smile, "she has them bronzed in her house as a symbol of her freedom.
"

"She sounds like quite the character. Very different from you, but friendships are often accents to our true selves."

"Yeah. *I miss her*. In the distance, I can almost feel what her mother felt when my mother died. Miss Sophia took it so hard she had a nervous breakdown. She sat in her house and cried for weeks," Quinn moistened her lips and shook her head, recalling that awful day.

"Maybe you can learn a thing or two from Sophia," Dr. Baker replied gently.

"I'm sorry?" Quinn furrowed.

"The death of a friendship is just as equivalent to the physical death of the actual friend," Dr. Baker crossed her legs. "You haven't spoken to Pandora in six months. You said she's expecting her first child any day now, so I'm sure you'd love to be there for support. Your husband is the love of your life and a former sex addict. One of his victims just so happened to be Joanna. Your marriage is broken, your home is broken, you haven't been involved in ministry, and your living situation forces you to be a part-time mother three days a week, yet, you're sitting in my office looking like Miss America. Your eye shadow isn't running, every strand of hair is in place, and you have a Kodak smile as you sit on my sofa conversing with me like we're reading the newspaper."

"I know," Quinn lowered her guilty eyes, "It's habitual for me to have it all together; even when it's all falling apart."

"Mannequin, you don't have *anything* together. You have to grieve," Dr. Baker reached over and touched her hand gently, "It is pertinent that you at least *cry*. Maybe not now, but at some point just let it happen. Don't choke it down. You need to either deal with your problems or release it so that your emotions can do what they need to do. But you *know* this, Dr. Bentley," Dr. Baker shook her head. "If you don't deal with your pain, this suffocating suffering you're doing will pass, and you'll be left with the pieces of yourself you destroyed in order to feel *nothing*."

Quinn stared out the window, refusing to respond. There was nothing she could say. She knew it was the truth. Was she ready to *face* the truth? That was the real question, and the answer to that wasn't something she needed a therapist for.

"How *is* your husband? Have you reached out to him?" Dr. Baker changed the subject.

"We communicate about the baby, nothing more," Quinn replied. "Early on he asked if we could talk about us, but I wasn't ready, so I declined. He hasn't asked since."

"Is he still dealing with the addiction?"

"He's sober, as far as I know," Quinn shrugged, "but then again, I don't know anything anymore. I'm unsure what to believe."

"May I ask what exactly it is that you want from your husband? You said he confessed and he apologized after he sought out a woman from your congregation. From an addict, that's what they're supposed to do, and it is often the hardest to do. And he did it. Why now are you torturing him with silence?"

"I'm not torturing him, I just—" Quinn's breath caught. Now that Dr. Baker said something, *why was she ignoring him*? "I'm still hurt. I'm still angry about what he did to my friend."

"Let's back up a little bit," Dr. Baker sat up. "A sex addict tends to get hooked on sex just like a drug and alcohol user."

"I'm aware of that."

"Those addictive sexual fantasies and behaviors trigger a hormonal release for them, resulting in feelings of pleasure, excitement, control, and distraction," She gestured with her hands. "This fantasy-induced neurochemical quagmire is a combination of dopamine, adrenaline, oxytocin, serotonin, and endorphins."

"And I'm aware of that," Quinn began to grow annoyed. She felt like her intelligence was being insulted.

"And so sex addicts learn to control and abuse their own neurochemistry in the same way that alcoholics and drug addicts learn to abuse alcohol, heroin, and cocaine. Their sexual activities can frequently go against preexisting values and beliefs."

"I'm aw-"

"You're *aware* of that, Dr. Bentley, I heard you, but do *you* hear you. You forgave your husband for an addiction that he otherwise could not control. You mentioned him sleeping with strippers and other things that were completely out of the norm for him. You understood this. He reached out to you for help, he got the help he needed, and you forgave him and went on to have a child. *Now*, because you find out your friend was a victim of his past addiction, you're reniging your forgiveness and taking two steps back."

"I did not renig anything," Quinn jerked her head back, appalled at the therapist's accusations, "I was *there* for my husband. My emotions were all over the place, but I was there, and I was faithful to him. Panic, fear, loneliness, hopelessness, confusion, anger, inadequacy, depression, and helplessness, you name it, *I felt it.* I was more forgetful than usual, I had trouble concentrating, and I couldn't stop the vivid thoughts. But I was there. I *never* left him."

"So why are you doing it now?"

"I'm not!" Quinn stood up as tears flew from her eyes, "I'm allowed a reaction. I don't have to lay here and take it. He cheated on me with a friend." "He cheated because of an addiction. But wait, didn't you mention infidelity on your part as well? Did he-"

"Alright, you know what? This session is *over."* Quinn roughly grabbed her purse and wiped her tears. Dr. Baker stood up.

"Mannequin, I'm sorry if you feel I'm being a bit pushy. You are a doctor with the same education as me. All you've been doing these last couple of months is playing mind games to protect yourself. You are wasting *your* money and *my* time. I want to get to the heart of the matter, but I can't do that unless-"

"I have a slew of paperwork to get done. Thank you for your time," Quinn glared at the woman as if she were looking straight through her. Fixing her attitude, she turned and pranced out of Dr. Baker's office with an intent never to go back. She would deal with her life on her *own*. She walked up to the elevator just as it opened.

"Oh, hi First Lady," A church member got off.

"Hi," Quinn replied hesitantly. She wasn't expecting to run into anyone from the church today. The woman reached out to extend a hug. Quinn followed suit and smiled. "How are you, Cheryl?"

"I'm doing well, thank you. I'm headed to an appointment in Suite Four. We really miss you at church. Pastor said you were still trying to grasp everything that happened, and that's understandable. He also mentioned you were suffering from bouts of the flu." Quinn just smiled. "I'm sure you're juggling a lot with the baby and getting settled in your new office. Take your time. This is hard for all of us."

"I'll see you soon, Cheryl. Thank you." The woman nodded and turned down a corner as Quinn stepped onto the elevator. Juggling sounded so perky and positive. Most days Quinn found herself cleaning up what'd fallen and shattered rather than keeping anything *juggling* in the air. As the elevator navigated to the first floor, she thought about her to-do list and the fact that she was behind on the laundry and had a stack of bills to pay. She should also schedule Heaven's routine wellness visit and sign up for the mommy and me gym classes. *Juggling was a horrible analogy to describe her life.* Quinn walked out of the elevator, out the door and down the street, en route back to her office. She'd spent her lunch break with Dr. Baker and now realized she was running late for her twelve-thirty appointment. Reaching into her bag, Quinn checked the time on her phone. "twelve-forty, ugh." She tossed her phone back into her bag and began to put some pep into her step. Just as Quinn looked up, two big arms reached out and grabbed her shoulders to prevent a full-on collision into one another.

"Oh my goodness, I'm sor-" she froze when she realized it was her husband.

"There you are."

"Hi," Quinn looked at Andre confused, wondering what he was doing downtown.

"I just left your office looking for you. They said you were at lunch. I was headed to the Bonefish around the corner. That's usually where you eat," Andre smiled.

"Actually, I had lunch with a friend today, so I'm running a bit late for an appointment. Did you need something?" Her honest gaze met his for the first time in almost six months. Often times they communicated through text and did brief exchanges of a hello with Heaven, but they hadn't been this up close and personal in a long time. Andre took a moment to study his wife's eyes. Over the years, he labeled them grey. If he was feeling particularly poetic, he called them silver. Neither word did them justice. They were so solid and so bright, they looked like an exact lustrous color of a polished shard of metal. If you looked closer, as Andre did, you could see the swirls of glittering black onyx, and tinges of blue at the edges. They were pure. They were cold. *They were breathtaking.* At that moment, Andre remembered the woman he'd fallen in love with. He remembered the way Quinn's long lashes framed her eyes when she captured a target, turning them into stone. He recalled the way her full lips would curl into a bashful grin every time she did so. It was inevitable and certain that once he looked at Quinn, he couldn't look away. She kept him still and held his beating heart with one gaze. *He missed her. Nothing so pretty could possibly harm anyone, right?* As they spoke, Quinn studied her husband. At just over six foot five, carrying two hundred and thirty-five pounds of strength and muscle, Andre was gorgeous, and wasn't that just grossly unfair? He looked rumpled, tired, and mentally exhausted, but his almond complexion, full lips, and dark gaze still made him appealing. Her fingers itched to sweep the shine from his forehead and then linger, as she'd often done. Because touching Andre was *always* fun. His dark gaze swept over her. Sadness tightened her chest, even as resolve straightened her spine. Quinn wondered how they looked from the outside. A successful couple, she thought. Andre had an air of confidence about him. No one would be surprised to learn he ran an eight-figure megachurch. He was also tailored impeccably in khaki Prada. The Italian's *knew* what they were doing with a suit. Quinn was dressed in one of her business suits. It was California-inspired—less structured than a traditional suit, but with all the pieces. Her high heels clicked on the cement path. *What happened to them?* Their love was the foundation of their humanity. It was their rock, and it was where they'd built their empire. Together, they had all the elements of a happy life; a big church, a booming business, a beautiful daughter, and good friends, but somehow the pieces didn't come together the way they should have.

"Listen, I've been trying to reach out for months to talk about us, but considering our pride, it didn't play out the way I thought," Andre put his hands in his pockets. They'd exchanged months of brief texts. His had been along the lines of, "This space between us was needed. I'm angry and hurt by our actions. We should talk about it soon." Quinn's had been edited from, "Go screw yourself," to a more generous, "Fine."

"Can we schedule for sometime next week when you drop off Heaven? I'm running late for-"

"No, Mannequin. We need to talk," Andre placed a hand on her shoulder, "Not next week, not the week after. Today. *Right now.*"

"Andre, I have paid clients waiting for me. I really don't have time today," Quinn shook her head. She really did want to talk, but she needed a few days to get her thoughts together. The conversation they needed to have wasn't spur-of-the-moment-worthy. Immediately, she could tell Andre was getting upset at her response. His gaze met hers, his stare unflinching. She saw emotions flashing through his dark eyes, and none of them were soft or loving any longer. Reaching into his pocket he pulled out a paper.

"I filed for divorce."

Just like that. Quinn forced herself to keep breathing, to focus on the moment. Her eyes dropped down to the paper. She breathed slowly, staying in the moment because to leave it was to acknowledge that her world had just crumbled around her. For weeks, Quinn wondered what it would be like if she and Andre split up. She'd played with the D-word, but hadn't actually believed it. Not in a way that meant anything. For the first time, she stared down into the chasm that was divorce and wondered what would happen if she was *forced* to the other side. The words on the page seemed to taunt her, as if to say, *"May the force be with you." Aft*er twenty plus years, this was what they'd amounted to? Their love was supposed to last forever. Had forever come so soon?

She wouldn't cry. Not in front of him. When they were done, she would go back to her office and finish her day. But that night- *all bets were off.*

"Mannequin, I love you. I will always love you," he hesitated, "I tri-"

Quinn reached into her purse and grabbed a pen. Taking the paper from Andre, she searched for the line that requested her signature. She signed it, handed him back the paper, and dropped her pen back into her purse.

"Divorce granted," she gave him a cold stare. "Is that all? If so, I *really* have to get to my appointment." Andre felt his heart cave into the floor.

"That's all," his voice shook as he looked away, trying to conceal the sadness in his eyes. Deep down, Andre wondered if Quinn still loved him anymore. Living in the reality of what he'd done to Pandora, the bullet that nearly took his arm off, and the way he almost blew up in flames with his church, he began to second guess *everything*. Andre didn't feel like he had the ability to be a fun-loving, kind-hearted, romantic husband anymore. He didn't feel like a good father, a good pastor, or a good friend. Andre felt like God was paying him back for the damage he'd done, and he felt so unworthy. He felt as if his addiction had driven Quinn into the arms of another woman. He felt ashamed. He didn't know how to save them, and it appeared as if Quinn hated him. As a result, he did what he thought she wanted. He was finally letting her go. Considering her reaction to it all, Andre felt as if his feelings were right.

"Keep me informed about the paperwork. I'll see you next week during drop off." Quinn gulped down a discrete sob and kept her composure before walking away. Her heart broke into little tiny pieces as tears of regret blurred her vision. She wanted so desperately to turn around and call him back. To beg on her knees that she needed him and that they could fix things. Quinn wished she could erase her mistakes and start over fresh, but Andre apparently didn't love her anymore, so her thoughts were useless. It was over, and she helped kill them.

Quinn walked inside her office and chose the stairs over the elevator. As she hurried up the steps, it was as if her emotions sprinted behind her, forcing her to feel everything that just happened. *There was no way she could hide from this.* Quinn's legs weakened until finally, she exploded. Lowering herself to the floor, she dropped her head and gave in.

"*Baby,*" she choked out. Divorce was never on the menu. Surviving without Andre would be torture. Quinn collapsed onto her side and sobbed out her pain, gasping for her breath. She was angry, she was afraid, and she was heartbroken. *This wasn't the way things were supposed to go...*

Chapter 6

*"If you don't deal with your issues, your issues will
deal with you"*

Parrot Bay was a three-story building with outdoor
dining on its main level. Inside, there was a huge open bar
that many locals took advantage of to watch sporting events
and socialize. It was just after nine p.m when Eden and
Pandora made their way inside for a late dinner. They
bypassed the second-floor dining room and went up to the
top-floor eating area.

"Should we sit by the window?" Eden asked,
already headed in that direction. The big windows offered a
view of the Pacific Ocean. Today they were partially open,
allowing in the cool, night air.

"Perfect," Pandora responded, waddling behind her.
At nine months pregnant, Pandora's protruding belly
looked as if it would pop at any moment. Her face was
chubbier, her lips fuller, and her hands and feet were
swollen to capacity. Still, she was drop-dead gorgeous. Her
smooth, honey skin radiated a pregnant glow. Her chestnut-
colored curls resembled fallen leaves, browned and sleek
with the first rain of autumn as they frolicked at her
shoulders. Her light brown eyes were the exact shade of a
latte, and they sparkled as eyeliner rimmed her eyes,
making them stand out so much more. Her dimples were

like a get out of jail free card. Eden felt like they should've come with a warning label: *Dangerous! Will knock your world off its axis. Categorized as a weapon. Proceed with caution.* Pandora had an amazing maternity wardrobe of flowy dresses and belly hugging tops. Tonight, she turned heads in a stunning, yellow Hérmes dress. She was easily the most beautiful pregnant woman Eden had ever seen. Pandora took a seat at the table and Eden placed her bag on the floor next to the chair, settling next to Pandora. Instead of engaging in their usual small talk about how they were doing, a hungry Pandora passed out menus.

"Great. All they have for the special is the burger platter," Eden muttered in disgust, "Do you see it? If I get that will you eat my fries?"

"I will," Pandora agreed, "I usually get the protein plate here." Eden wrinkled her nose.

"You eat so healthily for a nine-month pregnant woman. When I was eight months pregnant, all I could think about was deep-fried sugar."

"It wouldn't kill you to think of deep-fried sugar now, either. You're a stick," Pandora laughed and poked Eden in the arm. "You should eat more. We'll split the fries."

"I really *should* be more health-conscious, actually. Maybe I'll just get the Greek salad." Eden's eyes scanned the menu.

"Oh Gosh, Eden. Eat the burger. *And* the fries. *And* the milkshake," Pandora leaned back in her chair. "Enjoy your metabolism while you can, because one day it's all going to hell."

"Stop it. You look great."

"Honey, looks can be deceiving. I feel like a Gorilla. I can't even remember the last time I saw my toes.

Bruce swears they're still intact, but I don't believe what I can't see."

"They are adorable little piglet feet," Eden glanced under the table with a laugh. "Here, I'll take a picture." Pulling out her cell phone, she snapped a picture of Pandora's toes and showed her. Pandora grabbed the phone in disbelief, staring at it with a slacked mouth.

"They look like they belong to Miss Piggy."

"A very cute Miss Piggy," Eden rubbed Pandora's hand, "stop traumatizing yourself. You look stunningly beautiful. You've been glowing for months."

"I think I'm just sweating to death." They both shared a laugh.

Eden watched Pandora smile. She was bright-eyed, good-spirited, and innocently graceful. And then she thought of Quinn. *The human Mannequin.* Quinn's hair was always a glorious tumbling mass of khaki-colored curls falling down her shoulders. Quinn wore expensive watches and elegant jewelry. She drove a BMW convertible, and Pandora drove a black Aston Martin. If Eden could pick, she'd want Quinn for a mother, and to be Pandora when she grew up. They both had such flawless exteriors for two women with *black hearts*. They appeared soft and vulnerable, *human almost*. It was hard to believe the innocent blood on both of their hands. Especially Quinn. Two days prior, Quinn sent a text message to Eden asking if she and Pandora could meet her at Parrot Bay for dinner because she wanted to talk to them. Eden was all for it, but considering the tension between Pandora and Quinn, she knew Pandora would decline. Eden agreed to dinner and spent the next five minutes lying to Pandora about it. She invited Pandora to dinner, leaving out that there would be a third wheel joining them. "Hopefully, Quinn could simmer the impending, burning match that would be Pandora's temper when she got sight of Quinn," Eden thought. Her job was to get them in the same space. *She'd done her part.* Eden missed their trio and wanted so badly for things to go back to the way it was. She only hoped it all didn't blow up in her face.

"Good evening ladies, may I start you off with some drinks?" A waitress approached their table.

"Water with lemon for me," Pandora confirmed.

"Make that two," Eden smiled.

"No problem. Do you'll need a minute to figure out your order?"

"I think I'm ready," Pandora looked over at Eden. "Have you decided what you want to eat, toothpick?"

Eden looked at her watch before glancing down at the menu again. She didn't want to order without Quinn. Quinn had told her nine o'clock, and it was going on nine-thirty. Where was she? It wasn't like her to be late.

"Um, I need a little more time. I can't decide yet," Eden lied.

"Sure," The waitress said.

"How much time do you need? There are only three entrees on the menu," Pandora looked down at the menu, confused.

"Uh oh, you may wanna put some pep in your step," the waiter giggled at Eden. "The pregnant woman is ready to *eat.*"

"I beg your pardon?" Pandora raised an eyebrow, looking up.

"Oh, no-no, I didn't mean it in a bad way," the waitress defended, "I just meant you were eating for two, so you were starvin-"

"Do I *look* like I'm starving?"

"Not at all- I jus- you look gorgeous. I couldn't stop staring at you when you walked in. I-

"There's no sincerity in your compliment at all," Pandora glared, "It sounds like your trying to pity me."

"Absolutely no-"

"Are you trying to pity me? Because I will scratch your eyes out. *I will*."

"I swear, I wasn't." The waitress was sweating at this point.

"Whoa, preggo," Eden intervened, "I'm sure you have the best intentions," she looked at the waitress and chuckled, feeling bad. "Talking to pregnant women can get really tricky. Especially one in the throes of serious hormonal upheaval. It's like navigating through a minefield."

"I'm so sorry," the young girl looked afraid, "I've never been pregnant before. I didn't mean to offend you."

"It's alright," Pandora's eyes got softer. "At this point in my pregnancy I'm so tired of hearing everyone's running commentary on my size, my cravings and my health that even the question, 'How are you feeling?' sends me into a silent rage."

"No worries. I'm gonna go grab your drinks. Hopefully, when I get back you'll be ready to order," she caught herself, "Or if not you can take all the time you need. We close at midnight."

"Sure," Eden chuckled as the woman walked away. As soon as she disappeared around a nearby corner, Eden darted her eyes at Pandora. "She's gonna spit in our food."

"And I would own this place," Pandora pursed her lips. "Actually, this reminds me of one of my clients. A guy got into a dispute with a local restaurant manager, and he still decided to stick around and have dinner. As he chowed down on his pork chops, he caught a whiff of an awful smell. He went back that night and stole the security camera footage to view the kitchen during that time. Turns out, the manager sautéed his pork shops in his feces," She chuckled.

"*Ew*, oh my goodness. I'm sure that was the end of *that* restaurant."

"No, but it was the end of the fecal matter eating guest. My client was the manager."

"Figures," Eden rolled her eyes, shaking her head.

"The security camera showed the man breaking in with a firearm as well, so he was charged with first-degree robbery and sentenced to seven years in prison. *Without parole*."

"Anna, how could you?" She gasped, clutching her chest, "He was the one being victimized."

"That's my job," Pandora shrugged, "It's never to judge anyone, only to defend them.

"And you live for this kind of deceit and manipulation. That's a shame."

"I did. Once upon a time," she paused. "Now, it's beginning to get old very quickly."

"Yeah, right. Since when?" Eden tilted her head.

"A few months, maybe. Take today for example. I had a horrible morning dealing with some misogynistic idiot from the bank who insisted on continually asking to speak to my supervisor. When I explained I was the CEO of the company, I think he had a seizure," Pandora paused, her brown eyes dancing with amusement. "I offered him a scanned copy of my business card, but he declined. Then I told him that if he didn't get his act together, I would be moving the company's four-hundred-million-dollar account to another bank." She paused for dramatic effect. "I think I made him cry. And then this afternoon I received a call from a bargain-brand Hannibal Lector who ate his mother and father and spared the family dog. He insisted I represent him. For the first time, I felt wrong and I declined his case." Eden jerked her head back in disbelief.

"Say what?"

"I declined to represent him," Pandora paused to take in her response as if she herself couldn't believe it. "You know, in my ten-year career as a Defense Attorney, I have won seventy-three cases and lost one. Those are record-breaking numbers that used to be a badge of honor that I wore proudly." she looked down and smiled at her belly. "*And then he happened.* And everything's changing in my world, and it's much harder for me to be heartless and careless." Pandora looked up at Eden. "Next week is my last day in the office. I stepped down as the CEO and Attorney." Eden furrowed, completely shocked.

"*You're serious.*"

"As a heart attack. My line of work is very time consuming and dangerous. I used to get a thrill out of being the top dog, but as my mind switches into mommy mode, suddenly it's not so exciting anymore. I never thought I'd have children, so I've never considered the safety of anyone else's life other than my own. And now here I am, Bruce and I, and little baby Bruce on the way. All the love him and I have for each other, we put it in this safe place here," she massaged her growing belly. "I always thought my dream was to be a lawyer. Now, it's a mother. I feel vitally alive and thoroughly a woman. How could I possibly live with myself as a person protecting the lives of criminals while my son has to walk these same streets? So, Bruce and I reevaluated our personal and professional goals, and I decided to step down." Eden's eyes were as still as a billboard, watching her best friend in all her vulnerable glory. All her life, Pandora was a beast. She sacrificed years of schooling, her pride, and her ego to prove to the world just how beastly she could be. She was the queen of protecting criminals. She had a passion for her line of work, she went to bed late and got up early. She walked through courtrooms like she owned them, and her attitude and sharpness had landed her the title as one of the top Defense Attorneys in the country. Eden never saw her doing anything else, but as she looked into Pandora's eyes, she saw something different. Underneath the hormones and stress of pregnancy *was a mother to be*. It is every mother's due process to sacrifice, provide, and protect their young, no matter what it cost them. Before Pandora's son had even made it into this world, she'd already made a big sacrifice. A selfless one. Eden smiled. *Motherhood looked good on her.*

"Wow," Eden looked on in awe, "So what's next? Are you and Bruce gonna get married and you turn into Suzy Homemaker?"

Pandora giggled. "We've talked about marriage, but we're not in any rush. All my life I've wanted this. I've wanted motherhood, I've wanted success, and I've wanted Bruce Steed at the forefront of it all. Now that it's happening, we're content for the time being. As for a Suzy Homemaker, *hell* no I would never be any stay at home mom. Are you nuts?"

"So what are you gonna do?" Eden asked.

"Well. I took on another position; one that gives me more money, half the hours, and none of the danger. In six months I'll be appointed as the new State Judge of Virginia," Pandora cheesed, finally letting out her secret. Eden jumped up and screamed.

"Shut the front door! Anna? Oh my Gosh, congratulations," she rushed over to swarm her friend with an embrace.

"I'm excited," Pandora gleamed.

"Judge Anna," Eden laughed. "Holy cow. Is Bruce excited?"

"Absolutely. He stepped down from his position, too. He applied for an intelligence analyst position for the FBI, so if all goes well he'll be the one piecing together the information for private investigators. No more doing the dirty work."

"This is beautiful. I never thought I'd see the day you two would find your happy ending. So, if y'all can have more children, are you gonna have another after this?" Eden narrowed her eyebrows.

"Maybe. We'll see how it goes," she blushed. Eden's mouth dropped open at Pandora's bashfulness and vulnerability. *Who was this new woman?*

"Oh, I cannot *wait* for Quinn to get here and hear th-," she caught herself. Pandora's face froze. Her smile vanished into thin air. "I mean- not that she's coming here, but-"

"Eden," Pandora's nostrils flared as she folded her arms.

"Alright," Eden sighed, letting the cat out of the bag. "Quinn asked us to come here. She wanted to talk to us." Pandora glared. Her eyes had gone from soft and loving, to tense and deadly without any attempt to try and mask it. Grabbing her purse, she stood straight up.

"Not cool at all. I'm out of here."

"Anna, wait." Eden stood up. She grabbed Pandora's hand, and Pandora snatched it back."

"Don't touch me. You lied to me and you set me

up."

"I did not lie," Eden winced in defense. "I said I wanted to have dinner. I just left out all of the details. Look, she's still our best friend."

"She's *your* best friend." Pandora went to walk down the steps, but Eden forcefully grabbed her hand and turned her around.

"She is *our* friend, and she wants to talk to *us*. Stop this madness, *now."* Pandora and Eden traded stares for a long second.

"I don't have anything to say to her."

"Well, she has something to say to you, so you don't have to talk, but at least listen to her. Just like you, I'm floored by everything that's happened, and the silence behind it. It's not like Quinn to act like this," Eden shook her head in denial. "Something is wrong. *Very wrong.* Something happened that day at the beach. The more that Diamond girl rambled, something woke up inside of Quinn. Something dark, and dangerous, and-" Eden shivered and closed her eyes against the memory. Just thinking of that night gave her goosebumps.

"It's been six months, and she hasn't tried to reach out to me at all," Pandora fussed, "I don't know what's going on, but I shouldn't be in the dark about it *this long.* She obviously isn't the Quinn we thought she was all of these years if she's afraid to face me."

"It's not just you. She hasn't been to her church either. She hasn't been to her house- she doesn't *have* a house. Andre filed for divorce, and both of them moved out. I don't even know where she's staying." Pandora stared at Eden with an unfocused gaze as her mind froze and her mouth slacked. *Divorce? Moved out?* "The scene from the beach scared the crap out of me, so I needed a minute to process and get back to reality. I also knew that her and Andre were recovering from the church bombing, so I kept things cordial for a few months. After a while, I started texting and calling, but she barely responded. That's not like Quinn. Something about her silence spoke volumes to me. Then one day I decided to pop up at her house, and there was a For Sale sign stuck in the grass." Pandora clutched her chest. "*Exactly*," Eden nodded. "I went down to the church and saw Andre, and he told me what was going on. He didn't get into details, just that they'd split up months ago and he'd filed for divorce. I was planning to reach out to Quinn, but ironically she sent me a text and asked us to meet her here."

Pandora was at a loss for words. Immediately, she felt terrible. She had no idea what had gotten into Quinn or why she didn't bother to reach out to her. Pandora felt like she was owed answers. Who was Diamond, and why did Quinn flip out and choke her to death? What happened years ago when Pandora was kidnapped, and how did Quinn know where she was locked away? Surely, Quinn didn't have anything to do with it? Did she? Pandora didn't know what to think or what to believe, but the more Quinn avoided reaching out to her, the more negative thoughts bounced around in her brain. What kind of friend was she? Pandora was with Quinn throughout her entire pregnancy with Heaven. She loved that little girl as if she were her own. She was there when Heaven was born, and she took her everywhere with her. Pandora was now pregnant with a miracle baby, and Quinn wasn't around to support her through *anything*. Did she care? Pandora cried many nights as she stared down at her phone and waited for a text or phone call that never came through. Pandora felt abandoned, angry, and heartbroken. She also missed

Heaven. She hadn't seen her Goddaughter in months. She didn't understand Quinn's selfishness, but she had no idea that her distance was due to her entire world falling apart. Pandora felt guilty. Maybe *she* should've reached out instead. Was Quinn alright? Where was she? Did she need anything? The woman who'd been there for *everybody* finally needed help, and didn't have *anybody*. Andre was her life; how did divorce come about? Was it because of what he'd done to Pandora? Was it because of Diamond?" Thoughts swarmed around Pandora's head like a tornado. Suddenly, Heaven walked out of the nearby bathroom. Her almost-two-year-old self looked around hesitantly at first until her eyes landed on Eden and Pandora. She smiled at them, shaking her hands with excitement. Immediately, she rushed to Pandora.

"Heaven!" Eden smiled. Tears instantly fell from Pandora's eyes as she dropped her purse and reached down to scoop her up.

"Hi, baby." Heaven's bright grey eyes found Pandora's and she laughed, as only a baby can; a sweet sound unblemished by the hurts of life. Pandora squeezed her tight. "Oh my goodness, I've missed you," she confessed, planting kisses all over her face. Heaven's little face glowed from a light within, as her miniature arms wrapped around Pandora's neck and held on tight.

"Heaven, you're getting so big," Eden smiled. She looked around for Quinn to come out of the bathroom, but no one appeared. "Where's mommy?"

"Mommy go night-night," Heaven's sweet voice responded.

"Night-night?" Pandora looked at Eden, confused. Eden stared at Pandora, and they both looked at the bathroom door Heaven had walked out of. They rushed toward the door with worried looks on their faces. Eden got to the door first and flung it open.

"Qui-" A sheer scream finished her sentence. Quinn was laid out on the bathroom floor, unconscious. An empty bottle of prescription pills rested near her limp hand.

"Oh my God," Pandora's body was frozen stiff with fear, and she almost fainted. Eden knelt to the floor to shake her in an attempt to wake her up. Pandora rushed out of the bathroom with Heaven in her arms screaming for help.

Chapter 7

Tears trickled down Quinn's flushed face as she walked toward the shower in the beach house she shared with her friends. All along the walls were pictures of herself, Pandora, and Eden during happier times. Joseph was in some of them. Andre was in a few as well, grinning like an idiot while Quinn kissed his cheeks with lips full of funnel cake powder. Stepping into the shower, her toes flinched as they graced the cold ceramic floor. She turned the nozzle on, releasing thousands of lukewarm drops that darkened her hair and trickled down her back. Quinn closed her eyes as memories of better days flashed through her mind. She remembered a time four years ago when they all vacationed in France. Ruby had just purchased her coffee shop and decided to treat everyone to a vacation. One evening they all lounged around outside by the hotel's swimming pool. There were people stretched out on inflatable floats, some were diving, and others watched several children play tag while the lifeguards looked on. The radio blared from the poolside while the Parisian sun began to set. Joseph teased Pandora for her poor French accent until she grew annoyed, eventually sending him flying into the water. Miss Ruby mentioned a visit to the Eiffel Tower, causing Andre to slide Quinn a devilish grin. Quinn returned the expression with a bashful smirk of her own as they both remembered an intimate moment years ago that they shared near the Tower. Eden walked around with her phone in the air looking for a signal to text her new boyfriend, Christopher, while Ruby cursed her out and threatened to shove the phone up her behind if she didn't turn it off and live in the moment. As Quinn thought back to that day, maybe they all should've taken Ruby's advice to appreciate the present moment of their situation. Instead of getting upset, maybe Pandora should've appreciated all the playful, harmless ways Joseph loved on his baby sister. Maybe she and Andre should've planned to re-experience their exotic moment at the Eiffel Tower, and maybe Eden should've listened to her mother, put her phone down, and indulged herself it what was. Maybe they should've all taken a deep breath, looked around, and given thanks for life, longevity, friendship, and the pursuit of happiness. Andre often preached about the swift transitions of life, and boy was he right. *It was amazing the difference four years could make.* How gut-wrenching it was to know that what was, wasn't anymore, and would never be again. Pandora would never get to laugh and joke with her brother again. She would never get the chance to see what a good father he would've made, or watch her nephews grow up. Whether fussing about something or laughing, Eden would never get to hear the sound of Ruby's voice again. And Andre, "my sweet, gentle giant. If anyone needs grace," Quinn thought as tears continued trickling down her face, "it's my Andre." Andre Bentley was the sweetest man Quinn had ever met in her entire life. He was big, strong, and ruled with an iron fist, but he had a soft spot for Quinn. When Olivia taught Quinn what to look for in a man, Andre didn't fit any of those qualities.

"You want a man with a good career, a Ph.D., and a residual income. He has to be a provider, and he has to take care of you. He can't come with a temper or an ego the size of Texas like most men. And you'd certainly want a

man who has had the stability of both parents," Quinn could hear her mother's advice. If she'd taken it, she would've never fallen for Andre; or any man on the face of the earth for that matter. Olivia taught Quinn to look for perfection, but Quinn found the exact opposite. Andre graduated from college with a Bachelors's degree in health. He started grad school but dropped out to do mission work with his parents. When they fell in love, he was still living at home with them. He couldn't provide for Quinn financially, he had a horrible temper at times, and a huge ego. But Andre loved Quinn for who she was. He accepted her and all of her imperfections. He held her hand through miscarriage, death, and infertility. He gave her the space she needed during grad school and suffered through nights without her in his arms. When both of his parents died in a plane crash, Andre went through a terrible depression, and Quinn was his saving grace. When Andre eventually became a pastor, Quinn became a psychologist, and together, they built an empire. They saved money together, tithed together, prayed together, created a life together, and purchased their first home together. Now, *it was all over*. To add insult to injury, Quinn had just been released from a hospital three days prior after a gut-wrenching suicide attempt.

To make matters worse, when she'd gotten home the night after Andre served her the divorce papers, there was a picture message from one of her clients. It displayed Andre and a random woman at a restaurant having dinner. The text read:

"I'm at Amaretto. So is your husband. I'm sure it's a business meeting of some sort, but she is way too close and it's making it look like something else."

"No. He wasn't at a business meeting. That bastard

was on a date with another woman. *Already*. How long had this been going on? Who was she? Was she the reason for the sudden divorce request? Quinn gasped at the picture and burst into tears. Through her tears, she speed-dialed her client's number. The heartbreak in Quinn's voice sent her patient over the edge. Quinn was the queen of keeping her personal affairs private, but she didn't have anyone to talk to at this point. She and her client sobbed together for a long time as they tried to comprehend the reality that such a beautiful young couple at the brink of their lives and careers, was gone forever.

"Thank God you found out *after* he asked you for a divorce and not before," Her client kept saying. But the chronological sequence of timing was only a small consolation to Quinn, who would have to live with a hole in her heart and a broken family for the rest of her life. *And what about their church members?* And then there was Heaven, whom, at the moment didn't even understand that she'd never get to feel the security of mommy and daddy under one roof again. Quinn's life was all one big mess. After rinsing herself off, she shut off the water, grabbed a towel, dried herself off, and took the walk of shame back to her bedroom. As she walked by the images on the wall a second time, she longed so badly to whisper at the photos of the past, in hopes that her former self and everyone else's would step out of the frames. But this wasn't Hogwarts or the playful bear hunt nursery rhyme that she often sang to heaven. She couldn't go around it, and she couldn't go under it; *she had to go through it.* Quinn sifted through drawers looking through her old clothes. She hadn't stayed at the beach house in nearly a year so she had no idea what old things she'd left behind. Finally, she stumbled on a pair of sweatpants and a tank top and put them on. After putting her hair into a messy bun, Quinn made her way downstairs to raid the fridge. Her mind had been in shreds over the last three days, and she hadn't eaten much of anything. She expected to be dead and gone by now, but death never happened. She was supposed to be on her way to hell, instead, she found herself at her old beach house recovering from an opioid overdose. Quinn remembered walking into Parrot Bay with an intent to apologize to her friends, and then vanish into a suicidal death. But as she got to the restaurant, grief and guilt met her before Eden and Pandora did. After hiding behind years of facades, Quinn felt ashamed. She was embarrassed and broken beyond the ability to be repaired. Not only that, but she felt like a false prophet. Her and her husband professed the gospel of Jesus Christ to over three thousand members every Sunday. They traveled the world preaching about the effects of sin, while her husband struggled through a sex addiction, and Quinn was out *cheating* herself. She *cheated* her friends through secrets and half-truths. She *cheated* her daughter out of a mentally healthy mother, and she *cheated* on her husband with a woman she'd gotten romantically attached too, and then *murdered* her with the same hands she used to pray for others. Quinn stood in the restaurant bathroom warring with her mind until it all became too much. She opened a bottle of pills and swallowed all of them. Quinn waited and waited for death to come, but it didn't show up as instantaneous as she'd hoped. Instead, it was extremely unpleasant and scary. She remembered falling in the bathroom, rotating in and out of consciousness. Eventually, she heard screaming and crying from what sounded like Eden and Pandora. Then, *everything faded away*. When she awoke, she was tied down to an ICU bed with tubes and lines stuck in all types of uncomfortable places. Her stomach was being pumped, and her body had been injected with saline and medication to cleanse her liver. In Quinn's attempt to die, all she did was inflict horrible and unbearable pain onto the ones who loved her; *Pandora and Eden*. After being released from the hospital, Eden and Pandora drove to their beach house. Eden drove Heaven back to Andre, keeping a tight lip on the current events of his soon to be ex-wife's condition. She and Pandora stayed at the house by Quinn's side, just sitting around in silence. Quinn hadn't eaten, spoken a word, or gotten up to do much of anything other than using the bathroom. She watched her friends day and night, as they curled up on the bed beside her, talking amongst themselves until they eventually fell asleep. Eden had become such a woman over the last six months. She dyed her hair, took over her mother's salon full time, and was knee-deep in her graduate school studies. *And Pandora*. Every time Quinn looked at Pandora, she wanted to cry. Pandora was pregnant, glowing, beautiful, and Quinn had missed out on all of it. After Diamond ran her mouth, she knew Pandora was confused, angry and probably downright scared of what could have possibly been the truth, yet she put her pride aside to come to Quinn's rescue. Through it all, Pandora was always loyal. Reaching into the fridge, Quinn found pizza from the previous night that the girls had ordered for dinner. Eden had left for school and Pandora had gone to work, so Quinn decided it was time to get up and face the horrible mess she'd created. She couldn't stay in bed forever. She grabbed a slice of pizza, put it on a plate and opened the microwave. Just as she went to press the timer, the back door opened and Quinn's heart almost stopped. She spun around to see Pandora standing in the doorway. Both of them gasped through widened eyes.

"Oh my Goodness," Pandora clutched her chest, trying to calm her racing heart, "you scared me half to death."

"I'm sorry," Quinn's eyes met hers. "I was just coming down for some food." A silence filled the room as both of their eyes locked on one another. Quinn thought Pandora was working, and Pandora thought Quinn was confined to the bed. An unexpected run-in in the kitchen wasn't how either of them prepared to be reacquainted.

"Well- I'm. It's good that you're up and moving," Pandora walked in, slowly shutting the door behind her. She walked over to the counter where Quinn stood and put her briefcase down.

"...Yeah," Quinn hesitated. She stared into Pandora's eyes and grimaced at the beautiful soul staring back at her. Every time Pandora faced the world and all that it demanded from her, she was a lioness, but to Quinn, she was simply just, *Anna.* Pandora's humanity stared back at Quinn as if lighting a spark to the burnt out match that had been Quinn's life. Although confused, hurt, and angry at the events of the past, Pandora loved hard. *There was something about genuine love that had the power to bring every dead thing back to life.* Simultaneously, they both reached for one another, melting into an embrace.

"I'm so sorry," Quinn whispered, tears tearing from her eyes.

"I'm just glad you're alive," Pandora squeezed her friend as tight as she could. "I didn't know what was going on. I didn't know you needed me." Quinn's tears soaked Pandora's shoulder as her misery worsened. Her pain came in agonizing waves, leaving Pandora breathless. Her heart broke for her friend as tears fell from her own eyes. Quinn was always on the receiving end of someone else's pain.

She was always *their* answer. Now *she* needed an answer. After finally recovering, both of them walked into the living room. Quinn helped Pandora waddle to the sofa, before sitting down next to her. Pandora grabbed a Kleenex and wiped away Quinn's tears.

"You look so beautiful pregnant. I'm so sorry I wasn't there for you," Quinn shook her head as guilt filled her eyes.

"It's okay; you don't have to keep apologizing." Pandora wiped away her own remaining tears. "What matters now is you being alive. Quinn, you scared the *hell* out of us. I almost went into labor seeing you on that bathroom floor like that. Why is it that you and Eden have to wait until *I'm* around to decide y'all want to kill yourselves?" They both laughed through their emotions, lightening the mood.

"Listen," Quinn grabbed Pandora's hands, "I've hidden certain parts of myself from you and Eden for so long. It's been a habit of mine since I was little, you know? My mother used to always tell me that a pretty face can hide so much," she choked on her words. "And it did, and I hate it, and I can't do it anymore. And I'm sorry. This epic performance has been a huge drain on my mind, body, and soul."

"But why, honey?" Pandora asked, "It's a hard act to constantly pretend to be, or feel like you need to be someone else. Did you learn nothing from Jackson?" she giggled.

"I'm not sure. I think I've just always tried to be everything to everyone to prove that I was enough. Right now my own troubles feel big, and my faith is so small. I can't take another step."

"And you don't have to," Pandora wrapped her arms

around Quinn. "Let those who love you, carry you. You've always been a source of love and support for Eden and me; now you have to let us extend it back to you. Tell us your fears, your hurts, your struggles. It's okay to have weak moments, you're not Jesus," Pandora stared at her, her eyes laced with genuine concern. "We care about you, and we want to help."

"There you are. I thought you escaped," Eden rushed into the kitchen with a sigh of relief the minute her eyes landed on Quinn.

"Here I am," Quinn faced Eden, partially smiling through her red puffy eyes and frail face. Eden just stared at her like an alien for a brief moment. She'd never seen Quinn so disheveled before. "Yes, I'm a *train wreck.* Stop judging me and come hug me," Quinn chuckled. Breaking herself out of her trance, Eden rushed over and sat down on the other side of Quinn. She had so much to say, but she couldn't find the words. All that managed to come out was

"I love you," she nuzzled in for a hug. Today, the voices of her friends soothed Quinn and resuscitated her life. When it came to their souls, the three of them were aligned in ways in which neither of them understood. They were such an unlikely trio, Eden, Pandora, and Quinn, but they *worked* for one another. Quinn's frosty gray eyes landed on Pandora while she felt the warmth of Eden's gentle embrace, and at that moment everything seemed to simmer into a state of tranquility. Quinn's unsolved puzzles felt completely flawless, as if she didn't need to go out of her way to find all the other pieces. Sitting in the room was just the three of them- spirited away by all the cruel in the world. And it was perfect.

"Andre and I are getting a divorce," she swallowed, breaking through the silence."

"Is it because of what he did to Pandora?" Eden asked. Quinn wasn't sure how to respond.

"It is because of a lot of things," she admitted. "You know, when I was little, I always thought marriage was this magical happily ever after. I loved to dream about who my husband would be someday; until *someday* turned into the *present day* and I had to reconcile my expectations with my reality. Marriage is not a fairy tale. It's beautiful, but it's hard work, it's commitment, and it's often full of surprises. Two years ago, Andre came home from church one night," Quinn moistened her lips and dried her tears. "He was usually always happy and excited to see me. He'd tell me everything that happened at church, and who had gotten on his nerves. That particular night, he wouldn't even look at me. I asked him how church was, and he lashed out at me as if I'd done something wrong. He slept in another room away from me for the first time in ten years. I didn't know it then, but he'd secretly been battling a sexual addiction since college, and after nearly ten years of being in remission, that succubus spirit was getting ready to attack him again."

"No," Eden was shocked. "He has a sex addiction?"

"Yeah," Quinn responded faintly as if she herself still couldn't believe it. Pandora looked stone-faced. Quinn's statement was so out of character, and so far from what she knew of Andre, she just stared openly. Her brain formulated no thoughts other than to register that she was shocked.

"My dad fought with that spirit for years. It changed him so much that it wrecked his marriage with my mom and ruined his life. But Andre? How does that happen to a pastor?"

"A pastor is just a label, a gift, or a calling, rather.

He's *still* a man. He's still human. The Bible says that we wrestle not against flesh and blood, but against rulers and principalities in high places. The toughest battles we'll ever fight in our lives won't be against each other, but against the principalities of hell. Jealousy, envy, lust, bitterness, those are all spirits, and it doesn't matter how much money you have, or how popular and well-liked you may be. It doesn't matter if you're religious, spiritual, or the lack thereof; *we will all fight a demon at some point in our lives*."

"I knew a guy in law school who was a huge sex addict," Pandora recalled. "Everything about him was sexual. He ate, slept, and breathed orgasms. So much so that he could never formulate any lasting relationships because he'd always cheat. I assumed he was just a big hoe. Actually, when you think about it, a lot of men are like this. I never knew there was some type of spirit attached to it."

"Whenever you see or hear of anyone battling any type of addiction or struggle; it could be alcohol, eating, drugs, killing, whatever- there's always a tormenting spirit at the root of it all," Quinn responded. "A succubus is a type of spirit behind a sexual addiction. It lurks around in places where perversion is usually running rampant. Strip clubs, brothels, prostitution corners, certain movies and explicit TV shows, certain types of music that entertain perversion, lust, and cheating. It attaches itself to men, women, *anyone* that finds these things fun and entertaining. The issue is, we live in a sex-crazed culture where perversion *is* entertaining. It's accepted, embraced, especially by young boys trying to find themselves. People who fall victim to sexual spirits end up with a sex drive that is abnormally intense and often times dominates their lives. It becomes an itch they'll never be able to fully scratch.

They'll sleep with strippers, prostitutes, people of the same sex. They won't be able to stay in committed relationships; they'll masturbate a lot, watch crazy amounts of porn," Quinn shook her head. "For Andre, he got caught up with the Coach's cheating wife in undergrad. That one encounter created an uncontrolled addiction that ruined the next 15 years of his life. It was so uncontrolled at one point, he stole a moment that belonged to his best friend and took advantage of a young girl he viewed as a sister." Quinn looked at Pandora, and Pandora lowered her eyes at the confession. An eerie silence filled the room. It laid on Pandora's skin like poison. It seeped into her blood and temporarily paralyzed her brain. Suddenly, everything made sense to her. *It didn't make it right.* But it made sense. Eden rubbed her neck and looked away as well. She felt terrible for Andre and terrible for Pandora. "Still," Quinn's shaky voice pierced through the silence, "What he did to you wasn't right." Quinn lifted Pandora's chin to face her, "It wasn't okay, and it wasn't fair. When he told me about the addiction, suddenly, the cheating and the baby accusations made sense. I was hurt, but I tried to forgive him, and I couldn't. I love him. I didn't want to lose him, but I didn't know how to look past that. So, we fought and argued until we couldn't live together any longer and we separated. And now, here we are." Quinn bit her lip and forced herself not to break into the screaming cries that wanted out of her. "I have gone six months without my husband, and I'm not sure that I can make it to forever."

Quinn sat back on the sofa and fanned her face, trying to get herself together so she could finish her story. Pandora opened her mouth to speak, but nothing came out but a faint gasp. She was so heartbroken for Quinn.

"This is horrible," Eden winced. "There's got to be

a way to fix this. You guys were *made* for each other."

"It's not. He was out on a date with some other woman a few days ago."

"What?" Eden and Pandora gasped in unison.

"He doesn't want me anymore. As if he weren't broken and exposed enough, once he found out about Diamond, that was it for us."

"Well, what about Diamond?" Eden asked, confused. "Who is she? Where did she come from? That whole situation out by the beach scared the hell out of us. *You do know* you killed her with your bare hands, right?" she darted her eyes, reminding Quinn in case she was too out of it to remember. Quinn looked away and nodded her head slowly. "And then Anna picked up the phone and called these people who came and dumped her body in the ocean and fed her to the sharks." Just thinking about it again made Eden's skin crawl. "You know, I thought it was just Pandora, but both of you are completely nuts, and neither of you seems to care." Pandora rolled her eyes around in her head. Quinn looked away for a long moment before finally turning back to face Pandora.

"Diamond said something to you at the beach. Something that, before I tell you how I knew her, I have to tell you this first," she swallowed. "And, if after I tell you, you find that you hate me and you never wanna be friends with me again, I understand." Eden raised an eyebrow. Pandora sat back on the sofa and lifted her eyes to meet Quinn's.

Chapter 8

Junior year of High School; Virginia Beach, Virginia. 1999

Quinn and Andre sat on the porch steps of Quinn's four-story home by the waterfront. Andre sat on the top step while Quinn rested on the second landing between his legs. Andre played with Quinn's soft curls, periodically leaning down to plant kisses on her cheeks.

"Can't you just pretend like you're sick?" Quinn pleaded. "Two days is a *long* time."

"I wish. I don't want to leave you either," Andre replied, "but my dad keeps pushing me to be a Deacon, so he's pushing me to go to the Deacon retreat this weekend."

"But it's all the way in Baltimore. And for two whole days?" Quinn pouted.

"Come on baby," Andre stroked her cheek, "Don't make me feel worse. I can't tell my parents no."

"What time are you leaving?"

"In about an hour or so. We're just waiting for my mom to get back from the hair salon." Two days in Baltimore, Maryland felt like an eternity to fifteen-year-old Quinn. She and Andre hadn't been separated for more than a few hours. After a long week of SAT prepping, Quinn was more than ready for the weekend. Herself, Pandora, Bruce, and Andre were set to go double dating. They'd gone on dates in the past, but due to their curfew being eight o'clock, there was never any time for them to do much other than grab a bite to eat and hang out on the Pier. The four of them begged their parents for weeks to extend their curfew so they could all hang out longer. It didn't work. Olivia nearly choked on her spit at the thought of her only daughter running the streets of downtown Virginia on a Friday night, unsupervised. Guilda and Bruce's mother gave their sons a big fat "no" as well. There was too much trouble lurking around downtown just *waiting* for little boys to get into. Pandora's mother denied her request as well, however, if everyone else's parents had agreed, Pandora planned to sneak out of the house. A successful parent/teacher conference at Virginia High School changed all four of their parents' minds. Quinn had made the honor roll, Pandora was excellent on the debate team, and Bruce and Andre were so good on the football team, they were being scouted by Division One college coaches. As a reward, their parents finally agreed to a curfew extension. Quinn, Andre, Pandora, and Bruce leaped for joy. They couldn't wait to stay out late. Two nights before their double date was set to happen, Andre was forced to cancel due to a Deacon retreat all the way in Baltimore, Maryland. Quinn was crushed. Come Friday night, she expected to be in the back of a movie theatre sitting next to her best friend, while making out with her boyfriend. Now, she'd be stuck as a third wheel. Quinn considered asking Eden to go, but there was no way Miss Ruby would let Eden out of her sight at such an hour on a Friday night.

"I'm gonna miss you," Quinn tilted her head to eye her boyfriend. "I really don't want to be a third wheel with Anna and Bruce tonight."

"That's alright. One day soon, we'll have the ultimate date. It's gonna be our wedding."

"That's a long time from now."

"No, it's not. We're fifteen. The legal age for marriage is eighteen as long as our parents agree to it."

"And what makes you think my dad would ever agree to me getting married at eighteen?" Quinn giggled.

"True." Andre's eyes lowered for a split second before lighting up. "Well, we could always convert to Islam. Muslims can marry at sixteen. *Without parental consent.*"

"Islam? Your parents would kill you, Andre," Quinn chuckled.

"That's fine. As long as I die with you as my wife it'll be worth it," Andre smiled.

"Alright Romeo and Juliet," Olivia walked out the front door with a freshly baked apple pie in her hands. "There will be no death or Islamic conversions in the name of love."

"I was just kidding," Andre stood up nervously, stuffing his hands into his pockets, "Don't tell my parents."

"Cut my grass next week, and we've got a deal," Olivia winked with a smile.

"Deal," Andre smiled back.

"How did you hear our conversation with the door closed?" Quinn stood up. "I have no privacy, ever."

"I have eyes and ears everywhere, my dear," Olivia replied, staring at her watch. "Are you ready to head to Sophia's? I want to get there before this pie gets cold. She likes it hot and toasty, so she doesn't have to microwave it."

"I'm ready." Quinn looked at Andre as a feeling of sadness came over her.

"I'll see you when I get back, Quinn." Andre reached out and hugged his girlfriend.

"Back from where?" Olivia's eyes narrowed.

"I'm going to Baltimore with my parents for a couple of days. I'll be back on Sunday."

"Wow. That'll be fun," Olivia wrapped her free arm around her sad daughter. "They have excellent seafood. Bring us back some clams."

"Yes ma'am," His posture stooped as he looked at Quinn one last time before turning and walking away. Quinn watched Andre hop down her front steps and eventually disappear around the corner.

"My life is over," tears clouded Quinn's eyes.

"You've got to be *kidding me*," Olivia's lips parted. "He's going to Baltimore for *two days*. It's not the end of the world."

"Right. First, it's Baltimore. Next, it's a different college. Then what? The NFL? This is the first step of our love drifting apart." Quinn stomped down her front steps muttering something that sounded suspiciously like profanity, but Olivia couldn't be too sure, so she just stood there with a blank stare, looking at Quinn like she was crazy."

"And I thought *I* was bad when dad and I dated in college. This takes the cake," she followed Quinn down the steps of their captivating four-story home that sat on three acres of land. The Gray manor was so breathtaking it looked like it had been cut straight from an architect's magazine. Everything was geometric, which is usually the frame of everyone's home in VA beach, but this one in particular; you couldn't help but notice it. The roof was flat, and the door was just as wide as it was tall. The windows were taller than a man and took up the entire brick siding with polished steel beams that broke them into yet more rectangles. The look would've been entirely metallic like a mini downtown skyscraper had it not been for the cedar beams of the external porch, and the matching raised plant beds that contained only white blooms. Many of the local kids rumored Quinn's house to be a government base. Sometimes when they were out riding with their parents, they'd beg to pass it and then file past looking out the corners of their eyes because they didn't want to turn their heads and gawk. Around the house were more polished concrete paths, patios, and planters. It was speculated that their roof had a helipad, and in the garage was an armored Bentley; if such a thing existed, *it would be there.* As the only child of Olivia and Steven Gray, Quinn was blessed. The backyard was lovingly paved and full of land. The Grays had chickens, cows, and horses. Quinn followed her mother to her car. Just as Olivia pulled out her car keys, she glanced down at her still downtrodden daughter."

"You know what? How about we walk the block and a half to Sophia's? The fresh air will cheer you up."

"Sure," Quinn muttered. Olivia placed her keys back into her purse, and they both began walking.

"Honey, please cheer up. I promise it's not the end of the world."

"That's easy for you to say about something you don't understand."

"Yes, because I was never fifteen before," Olivia rolled her eyes in amusement.

"You and dad met in college. You were older. Things were different. Andre and I have been together since middle school. Next year, we'll be seniors in high school," Quinn walked beside her mother. "We have plans on being together forever, and his parents are *ruining it.*"

"That's one of the first things that come out of young people's mouths when they're in love. *Forever.* And then one day my dear, you'll be old enough to realize what forever is. I was in love once, around your age. Long before I knew your father existed."

"Really? Then why do you always brag about Dad being your first love."

"That's because I don't really like to talk about it," Olivia moistened her lips.

"Tell me," Quinn's eyes lit up.

"I will tell you if you promise you'll cheer up and understand that Andre isn't going anywhere. You'll have a mature, sturdy bond that is delightfully intriguing," Olivia grinned, "love loves its youth, and if you can hold on to that innocence, you'll *never* have to worry about straying away from each other."

Quinn took a minute to think about her mother's words.

"I promise," She affirmed with a head nod. "Now, tell me about this mystery man that no one else knows about."

Quinn was excited. She often shared secrets with her mother, but this was the first time Olivia had a secret of her own.

"I had a friend that I'd known since forever. I think we may have been about two, three years old when we met. Just like you and Andre, we went through grade school together."

"What was his name?" Quinn asked.

Her mother thought for a minute before answering.

"Wilson," Olivia chuckled. "We fell in love at twelve years old. We were an unlikely couple. Total opposites. I came from a wealthy, healthy family, but Wilson came from an Orphanage. Needless to say, my parents were alright with us being friends, but they certainly wouldn't have accepted us being together.

"But why?"

"Well," Olivia thought, "now that I think about it, I'm not too sure. That's just the way the world works. My family had a vision of who they wanted me to grow up to be. In love with Wilson wasn't one of them. As a result, we kept our love a secret, and it was the best-kept secret ever. Wilson made me laugh, made me cry, and held my hand when I needed it. We'd go to school and make out in the boy's locker room during lunch and recess. Sometimes we'd ditch last period and find a broom closet to kiss in. Wilson was like the plague, and all I ever wanted was to be infected." Quinn burst out laughing, watching her mother blush. "You're laughing; I'm serious. I was so in love. When I was younger I had a few boy crushes, but nothing like this. Wilson would look at me, and I would melt like ice cream on a hot summer day. And because our time together was always limited and secretive, we cherished it and made the most of it."

"So what happened to him?"

"Well, as we got older we grew tired of sneaking around. We were grown and getting ready to graduate school and head off to college. How our parents felt about us didn't really phase us anymore. We both planned to run off and get married the minute we turned twenty-one. But it never happened. After seeing the woman I'd amounted to, Wilson didn't measure up and was afraid of how it would look."

"So he dumped you?"

"More like started another family and had a baby on me."

"What?" Quinn gasped.

"Yeah," Olivia replied with a somber glow, "I guess it just wasn't meant to be, so we parted ways. Shortly after Wilson, I met dad and the rest was history." Olivia's dull eyes began to water. She quickly wiped away the onset of tears before Quinn saw.

"Mom," Quinn took her hand, "You're crying."

"I'm not crying," Olivia forced a soft laugh to mask her emotions, "I had something in my eye."

"You know, for a long time, I'd see that same sadness in your eyes, and I never understood where it came from. I was always too afraid to ask because I thought you and dad may have been fighting. But now I get it," Quinn gave a condescending smile. "You're still in love with your first love."

"I don't know what look you're referring to. I'm perfectly fine," Olivia lied. "I did at one point, think about what could've been, but if what I wanted would've happened, there would be no you." Olivia squeezed her daughter's hand. "I'd suffer a million years of heartbreak if it meant I could still have my baby girl."

Quinn smirked. "Does dad know about him?"

"Of course he doesn't. No one knows. The only person I've ever told was Soph. And now you."

"Did Mrs. Sophia ever meet him?"

"Plenty of times," Olivia sniffed, getting herself together. "Anyway, the moral of my story is that sometimes you have to believe in your heart. You and Andre have love. That love cannot be quantified, and it is incomparable. You both love in the way puppy's love. Devoted, playful, and trusting. Andre never leaves your mind, he's always there. There will be times where he'll have to go away, and there may be times when you'll have to go away, but as long as you remember this love," Olivia pointed at her daughter. "This innocent, endearing, young love; you'll make it."

"I will," Quinn listened intently to her mother as they reached Sophia's house. She felt better about Andre going to Baltimore now, and maybe if he had to go away again, she wouldn't be as emotional. Quinn and her mother walked up the steps to Sophia's door. Just as Quinn stepped up to ring the doorbell, the front door swung open.

"Finally," Pandora sighed with excitement, happy to see Quinn. "What took you so long?"

"Anna!" Quinn smiled. They both hugged as tightly as they possibly could.

"Quinn, I have to show you my outfit for tonight. My mom made it for me." Pandora pulled Quinn's arm as they both rushed into the house leaving Olivia standing there holding her Apple pie.

"Don't mind me. I guess I'll just let myself in," Olivia shook her head with a smile.

"I'm sorry," Pandora spun around and rushed out to greet Olivia with a hug. "Hi. Mrs. Olivia."

"Hello, Anna."

"Oh, is that your famous apple pie?" Pandora's eyes widened.

"It is," Olivia walked in the house, shutting the door behind her. "Your mother told m-" Her words were cut short by screaming coming from upstairs.

"I told you about spending so much money!" Big Joe screamed.

"Joseph, it's thread. I have to make a prom dress-"

"Shut up while I'm talking!" A loud slap followed.

Pandora and Quinn looked toward the stairs, terrified. Olivia quickly sat the pie on the living room table.

"You girls go ahead and look at Pandora's outfit," she motioned for Pandora and Quinn to go into the next room. They quickly obeyed. Olivia walked toward the top of the stairs just in time to see Big Joe rushing down screaming.

"I want my money back, Sophia! And I want it back by the time I get ho-" He reached the bottom of the stairs and froze when he saw Olivia glaring at him.

"Hello, Olivia," he adjusted his tone into a more respectful one.

"Joseph," Olivia glared back with eyes full of deadly promise. Olivia couldn't stand the very sight of Joseph, Sr. for the way he treated her best friend. Over the years, she tried talking Sophia into leaving him plenty of times, but Sophia was too weak to do it. Joseph didn't care too much for Olivia either, but he respected her and stayed out of her way considering her husband was a Judge. All it ever took was one phone call to Steven Gray, and Joseph would be dragged to jail.

"Soph is upstairs getting dressed. She and I were just handling some business. I'm going to my office for a little while. You ladies take care." He didn't even wait for Olivia to respond. He quickly shuffled to the left to get down the rest of the steps. Just before he reached the front door, Olivia spun around.

"One more time, Joseph."

"Stay out of our marriage, Olivia. You don't-"

"One-more-time," she threatened with a tone that told Joseph she meant business.

"Whatever," He replied with an attitude before walking out of the house and slamming the door behind him. Olivia shook her head and walked up the stairs to see her friend and to survey the damage he'd done. She walked down the long hallway toward Sophia and Joseph's master bedroom. Sophia was sitting at the foot of the bed with her head in her hands.

"Soph," Olivia called, walking into the room. Sophia looked up. Her face was full of anger, blended with a sharp taste of humiliation. It was also bright red from a slap to the face.

"Hey," Sophia's voice cracked. Olivia stood there and shook her head.

"Soph, how long are you gonna let him treat you like this?"
She walked over to her friend to see about her face.

"Liv, we were just talking," Sophia stood up, dodging
Olivia's touch.

"Looks more like he was talking to your face. You know
the girls are downstairs, and they heard everything." Sophia
opened her mouth to defend herself, but tears of guilt fell
from her face before she could respond.

"It's okay," Sophia choked down a cry, wiping her tears,
"its okay. Eventually, we'll get better."

"Hopefully it gets better before he kills you."

"Oh stop it," Sophia flagged her off. "Let's just drop it.
He's gone. I wanna have a good evening. I smell pie," she
forced a smile, changing the subject.

"I took it out of my oven and walked right over while it
was still warm." Olivia smiled.

"Oh good," Sophia walked over to her full-length mirror to
look at her face. "Why'd you walk? Something wrong with
your car?"

"No." Olivia walked over to Sophia's closet in search of
her makeup bag. "Quinn had a meltdown after Andre left."

"Left?" Sophia turned, "they broke up?"

"No. He went to Baltimore with his parents," Olivia rolled
her eyes.

"Oh Jesus," Sophia laughed. Olivia located the bag and
looked inside for Sophia's mascara. Taking it out, she
closed the bag and walked over to Sophia to apply it to her
face."

"Young love, honey," Olivia shook her head.

"That's the best kind."

"It is. I shared with her the story of Wilson and I."

"Who?" Sophia furrowed, genuinely confused. After a split second, her memory returned to her. "Oh. Wilson! Wow. That was ages ago."

"It was. I was so in love," Olivia smiled at the thought.

"I remember. Wilson loved you too."

"Yeah right," Olivia finished Sophia's makeup. "Love is an action word."

"And love is what flowed from both of you. It just wasn't meant to be. Besides, you have Stevie now."

"Right." Olivia walked away.

"Livi, come on. It's been years. Don't do this," Sophia followed, grabbing her arm. "You're married now. There's no sense in thinking about some old flame. Unless it's still burning." Olivia turned to face her friend with a face full of tears. Sophia's eyes widened. Shoot. There *was still a* flame.

"Livi," Sophia winced, as they both stared at one another. Suddenly, Olivia leaned in slowly, connecting her lips with Sophia's. Indeed, a flame was still burning for Wilson. *Sophia Wilson.* The minute Olivia kissed her ex-lover, Sophia's brain lit on fire and the warmth spread throughout her entire body. It had been years since they'd felt one another's lips. Olivia's kisses were Sophia's salvation and torment. She once lived for them and would've died with the memory of them on her lips. Quickly stepping back, Sophia forced their lustful greeting to an end.

"Olivia," Sophia breathed heavily, trying to get her hormones to behave.

"I love you. I miss you, and I still think about you every day," Olivia admitted.

Sophia turned her back against Olivia and fanned her face. "Tell me you don't feel the same way, and we'll ignore this even happened," Olivia's voice shook. Sophia couldn't respond. All she could do was face the wall in denial. She'd thought about Olivia and what they once had for the last *ten years*. Each day seemed to get worse.

"I love you, too," Sophia finally turned around. "I will always love you, and I will always miss you."

"So why are we playing these games?" Olivia threw her hands in the air. "Why did you do this to us?"

"I didn't do anything to *you*. I did what was best for *me*. Olivia, you're a doctor from a rich family, and I'm an orphan from the ghetto. Big Joseph is all I have. I can't just walk away and leave him, trying to chase love. I have children- I have a *daughter.*"

"Who cares? I'm a doctor for crying out loud! I'll take care of you. You can go out and finish school, you can get a job, or you can stay at home and sew if you want. I don't care what you do; I'm just tired of living a *lie*. I'm tired of living life without you."

"It's not that easy, Liv," Sophia shook her head.

"Why can't it be?" Olivia's eyes pleaded, grabbing Sophia's hand.

"Because- look at everything we've done to ourselves," Sophia snatched her hand away.

"*Ourselves?*" Olivia winced, "*you're the* one that got pregnant behind my back."

"Yes, after you introduced me to a womanizer and told me to date him as a decoy."

"I didn't know he was crazy. He was good friends with-"

"Well, he was, and I didn't find that out until one night of sex got me pregnant with little Joe. He practically forced me to marry him, and now I'm stuck here in this hell hole."

"Why did you even tell him you were pregnant? You could've gotten an abortion."

"So what? He could've found out and killed me? Are you crazy?"

"Are *you crazy*? You didn't just get pregnant once; you let him knock you up twice."

"Yes, and as a way to get back at me, you went and slept with some drug dealer at a strip club and got pregnant. And then you pinned the baby on poor Steven," Sophia gasped, still shocked at the nerve of her ex-girlfriend. "Do you have any idea what would happen if he ever found out you-"

"He will never find out. We're married. Why on earth would be ever suspect his *sweet, gentle Olivia* to lie to him?" she mocked herself, rolling her eyes. "I'm so tired of living a lie. Despite everything that happened, we were supposed to raise our children together, and we were supposed to *be together*."

"*And I considered it*...until I had Anna. I can't do this to her. Every day she watches her weak mother being pushed around and spoken to like a dog. If I don't do anything else right, I at least want to raise my daughter and give her a normal life. I don't want her knowing about us. She loves Quinn so much, and it would ruin their friendship. It would ruin e*verything*. The whole town would be in a ruckus."

Sophia looked at Olivia. "You would be willing to shake up Mannequin's perfect childhood over love?"

"Yes," Olivia responded without even having to think about it. "I'm willing to tell my daughter the truth, the whole truth and nothing but the truth. *For you*. For us. Living this big lie as if I'm happy, is me *lying* to my daughter."

"Well, I can't," Sophia shook her head. "Maybe things would be different if Anna weren't here. But I just can-"

Tears rushed down Olivia's face at yet another rejection.

"I have to go," Olivia turned around and stormed away.

"Olivia!" Sophia scolded, "stop running and -"

"Your pie is on the living room table. Quinn can stay here with Anna. I have work to do at home." She bolted down the stairs and out the front door. She could hear Sophia calling her name, but she ignored her. Olivia slammed the front door as anxiety curled through her. It twisted around her heart until she thought she'd die right in the middle of Sophia's walkway, but she forced herself to keep walking. After all these years, the pain still felt the same. Olivia and Sophia had been in love since they were twelve years old. Afraid of what anyone would think, they even dated boys, but always met up in secret. Sophia was content in their secret relationship, but Olivia always wanted more. She was sick and tired of the lies and games. Sophia had gone on to have two children, and Olivia herself had gotten caught up with a baby. Olivia hated that they'd brought children into this world the wrong way, but she refused to live a lie for the rest of her life. The minute Sophia gave birth to Pandora, she cut ties with Olivia as ever being any more than just *friends*. She wanted to be a good mother to Pandora and didn't want her baby girl to see her mother involved in that kind of lifestyle. Olivia didn't like the decision, but she had no choice but to live with it. Since the day Pandora was born, Olivia hated her with a passion. She refused to come to the hospital to witness her birth, and she refused to allow her daughter around her as they got older. It didn't matter to Olivia that both of the girls were around the same age; Pandora was a thorn in Olivia's side and public enemy number one in her book. Eventually, Olivia knew as their girls got older, they would end up as friends, but she held out as long as she could. As she stepped off of Sophia's front porch and began a fast-paced walk back to her house, a soft voice called her name.

"Hello, Dr. Gray," Mrs. Perkins smiled, sitting on her porch. Olivia stopped in her tracks and looked up, quickly wiping her face."

"Hello, Mrs. Perkins," She sniffed. "How are you?"

"I'm just fine. You look like you were crying. Everything okay?"

"Yes ma'am," Olivia smiled through her pain. "It's allergy season so my sinuses are acting up."

"Would you come inside for a second? My husband and I are having a hard time setting up our VCR. Maybe you can help us."

"Mrs. Perkins, I'm a doctor, not a technician," Olivia replied with a gentle tone.

"Would you please just come to see if you can help?" Mrs. Perkins pleaded.

The way she felt, Olivia really wanted to tell Mrs. Perkins to take her VCR and shove it up her behind. She was on her way home to wallow in her self pity, and the last thing she wanted to do was be bothered by the annoying elderly couple next door.

"Sure," She digressed.

"Thank you so much," Mrs. Perkins smiled, standing up. She walked into her home followed by Olivia.

"The TV is just upstairs in the middle room. My husband is up there, he'll show you."

"Alright," Olivia replied, annoyed. She made her way up the steps and down a long hallway. As she grew closer, she could hear familiar voices coming from the bedroom. Her eyes furrowed at the familiar conversation. *It almost sounded like herself talking*. Olivia entered into the middle room and saw a large television connected to a VCR that appeared to be working just fine. Playing on the screen in clear Technicolor was herself, Sophia, and the entire conversation they'd had in Sophia's bedroom a few minutes prior. Olivia froze, clutching her chest as her mouth opened wide.

"What in the-"

"Hello, Dr. Gray," Mr. Perkins walked up behind Olivia, causing her to jump to the side. "I'm sorry; did I scare you?" He smiled.

"What the *hell is this*?"

"That? On the television?" he pointed. "It's you and your lover," He smirked at her secret.

"Wha-" Mr. Perkins put a hand up.

"Before you say anything, just let me reassure you, there's no need to worry. Your secret is safe with us." Mrs. Perkins walked up the steps with a devilish grin. "I'm sure you have a lot of questions as to how we videotaped your conversation. Trust me, it wasn't intentional. My wife and I are actually interested in a young girl in that house. *Joanna.* And judging from the conversation we overheard, it looks like our interest in her would work out in *your favor*. With that being said, *we could use your help.*"

Chapter 9

It was just after nine p.m when Olivia walked somberly into her home. She'd worked forty-eight hours straight at the emergency room, and there wasn't a word yet created to describe her exhaustion.

"Mannequin?" She called in a barely audible voice, walking through her living room into the kitchen. She flicked on the light switch to the kitchen and to her surprise, everything was still in its proper place. There were no dishes in the sink or half-eaten potato chip bags left on the counter as Quinn usually left them. The barstools under the kitchen island were neatly under the table, as were her dining room chairs. Olivia had a cleaning company that cleaned her home every week. They'd come the morning she left for work on Monday. It was now Wednesday, and her home still looked immaculate. This meant Quinn hadn't been home. Reaching for her cellphone, she dialed her daughter's number. After the third ring, Quinn answered. "Hello?"

"Hey you," Olivia spoke cheerfully over her exhaustion. "I just got home. You're not here. Where are you?"

"I'm over Miss Ruby's," Quinn replied. She wasn't at all excited to hear from her mother.

"Have you been there the entire two days I've been gone?"

"Yes. Why would I stay in that big giant haunted house alone? Dad's not here anymore." Anger sliced through

Quinn's voice and went straight through the phone into Olivia's heart.

"Sweetheart, it's okay to visit Ruby and Eden, but you don't live there. You live *here*. This is the third time this month you've stayed the night out without telling me."

"Well, if you know where I am, why does it matter?"

"I don't like your tone," Olivia placed a hand on her hip. "You need to-"

"And I don't like that you're such a *liar and* now Dad hates us!" Quinn fussed.

"Mannequin, we're not gonna do this over the phone," Olivia threatened. "I've told you about your mouth. You will respect me; I don't care how you feel. Now, if you want to talk about it we can-" Before Olivia could finish her statement, a dial tone sounded in her ear. Looking at the phone, she shook her head and sighed before tossing it onto the kitchen counter. Part of her wanted to drive to Ruby's and drag Quinn back into the house, but it was pointless. Olivia was tired, she was scared, she was heartbroken, and fighting a fifteen-year-old angry teenager wasn't a battle she could take right now. Ignoring her grumbling stomach, she walked out of the kitchen with the intent to deal with her appetite later. Instead of climbing to the third story into her master bedroom, she walked back into her living room and sank into the couch. A thousand memories flashed through her mind as she thought about the recent events that had been her life. Two months prior, Olivia planned a function at the hospital for locals to donate blood. She begged her husband Steven to participate, but he hated needles and respectfully declined. Olivia had been campaigning at the hospital for months and was so excited at the many donors who'd signed up. At the last minute, Steven decided to support his wife as a surprise. Not only was he attending for support, but he'd talked himself into giving blood as well. He thought it would be an even better idea to have Quinn come. She needed community service hours as part of her senior project, so Steven figured she could get a head start on it. He picked Quinn up from school and went to his primary care doctor to obtain the necessary paperwork needed to give blood.

"What does 'blood type' mean?" Quinn sat in the driver's seat scanning through Steve's stack of papers.

"It's a classification of blood-based on the presence and absence of your antibodies," Steven replied. "It's also based on the presence or absence of different inherited antigenic substances on the surface of red blood cells."

"Wow, that makes so much sense, Dad," Quinn replied sarcastically.

"Ok, let me try it again. This time, on your level of understanding," Steven laughed. "There are different blood types that a person can have. They can have A, B, AB, or O. When we have children, we pass the letters off to them. It's always important to know your blood type for things like donating blood, surgeries, or transfusions as you get older."

"That's pretty cool," Quinn sifted through the forms. "It says here your blood type is A. What's moms?"

"Mom has A-type blood as well."

"And what about me?"

"I'm not sure; we've ever checked. However, you can only have a blood type combination based on what we've given you. If I have an A, and mom has an A, that means you can only be an A or an O.

"How can we find out?" Quinn asked excitedly.

"Whenever it's time for you to give blood, I guess. You're only fifteen...You'd have to wait until next year if you wanted to donate. Then we could find out.
"Come on, Daddy, I want to know. Can't we go by my doctors and look at my blood work from before?"
After thinking about it for a minute, Steven decided maybe it wouldn't be such a bad idea. Quinn's primary care doctor was only a few stoplights away from the hospital, so it wouldn't take that much time. As requested, he went into her doctor's office and paid the ten-dollar fee needed to obtain the results of Quinn's recent vaccinations and blood type. As he walked back to the car, Steven scanned through the forms, taking in a count of all the vaccinations she'd received as a child. He nearly choked on his spit when he saw his daughter had a blood type of *AB*. Steven didn't have a *B or an AB to* give, and neither did Olivia. *This meant one of them wasn't the parent.* After fifteen years, Steven Gray discovered in the most embarrassing way, that the daughter he raised didn't belong to him. As a judge, he'd seen so many cases where men had fathered children given to them under false pretense. Never in a million years would he imagine he'd be one of them.
"I told you I was pregnant," Olivia defended, "I never said you were the father."
Steven was so heartbroken. He packed his things, filed for divorce, and walked out. Steven loved Quinn more than life itself. Since birth, she'd been daddy's girl. Now? He couldn't bear to look at her. Not because he didn't love her or care, but she looked too much like her mother. After a month of debating on what to do, he chose to disappear for good. He left Olivia the house, the cars, and her daughter. He vowed never to speak to her again and prayed every day that she'd die a slow, painful death for what she did. Quinn

and her mother's relationship went downhill after that. Olivia tried masking the situation with more lies about how she was framed, but Quinn wasn't stupid. She saw the papers, and she saw her ex-father's heartbreak. This was such a depressing turning point in Olivia's life. It also didn't help that she'd secretly taken part in the successful kidnapping of Pandora, six months prior. It was never Olivia's intent to involve herself in such a thing. While she certainly had demons, she wasn't *evil*. The day she walked into the Perkins home she was met with an ultimatum to either help them secure a successful kidnapping, or the video that recorded her confession of her ongoing relationship with Sophia would be given to the media for the entire world to see.

"This is sick," Olivia winced in disgust, "Why the hell would you want to kidnap a child?"

"Mr. Perkins is deathly sick," Mrs. Perkins lied. "We need fifty thousand dollars to pay for a successful surgery that would save his life. We don't want to keep the child; we simply want her to go missing long enough for the government to issue a monetary reward for information that leads to her return. It takes about three weeks to a month. Afterward, we'll call in, give them details, they'll find her, and we'll get our money. She'll be safe and sound back with her parents, and you'll have Sophia right where you want her."

Olivia thought the whole plan was absolutely nuts, but she agreed in an attempt to get Sophia back. Sophia had a soft spot for her only daughter. A month without knowing where Pandora was would send Sophia into an uproar. She'd be crushed, and vulnerable. Big Joe could've cared less, which meant Sophia would be right where Olivia wanted her: *In her arms*. In Sophia's moment of suffering,

Olivia hoped that maybe Sophia would see how much she cared. Hopefully, once Pandora was found, Sophia would realize she was wrong about her decision to continue to hide their love and want to be together. It sounded risky, but at this point, Olivia was willing to do anything to get the love she'd lost, back. On the day of the kidnapping, Olivia created a distraction via a prom dress. She took Sophia out and talked her into buying the most expensive junior prom dress that Joseph's money could afford. She told Sophia that with all the money Big Joseph spent on Little Joe, Pandora *deserved to* have a beautiful prom. She was an A student, and at some point, Sophia should stick up for her daughter. Sophia listened to her friend and purchased the dress. She also got her shoes, jewelry, and a matching purse. About two o'clock that afternoon, Olivia walked into Joseph's bank pretending to be distraught. She went into Joseph's office and told him how Sophia went crazy and spent five hundred dollars of his money for a prom dress and accessories.

"I told her Anna didn't need that kind of costly dress for something as simple as a junior prom, but she did it anyway. And she used your hard-earned money. She also flirted with the clerk at the register after he offered to take her to dinner. If I were you, I'd get home now and remind her of who's boss. You know, I've always been on Sophia's side, but things like dignity, being frugal, and fidelity are still important to me. She is in public embarrassing you and you need to set her straight." Big Joe was so angry you could see the veins popping out of his forehead. "Just *please*, don't tell her I told you. I don't want to get inv-"

Joseph slammed his briefcase shut, jumped up from his desk and stormed out of the bank. By three o'clock that afternoon, Big Joseph was already home giving his wife the full, *distracted curse* out. Olivia knew with the kind of trouble she'd started, it would cost Sophia quite a beating, but in due time, hopefully, Sophia would be out of Joseph's hands for good. With the distraction set, Pandora came home around three-fifteen, and the Perkins' were able to successfully pull her into their basement without being seen.

After the kidnapping, everything Olivia thought would happen between her and Sophia had happened. Sophia blamed herself for everything. She assumed if she'd been a stronger wife and stood up for the truth, Pandora would still be here. All she ever wanted to be was a good mother. She'd failed as a wife, and now she'd failed her daughter. Every time she thought of what may have happened to Pandora, she cried. And Olivia was right there to pick up her broken pieces. The situation had brought both of them closer. Olivia was grieving the loss of the broken marriage she never wanted, and Sophia was grieving the loss of her child. Sophia regretted living a lie and thought maybe if she'd wallowed in her truth with Olivia from the beginning, things wouldn't have occurred like this. Olivia took some time off work and was there to lick all of Sophia's wounds. They cried together, prayed together, and stayed nights together. Things between them had gotten back to normal. Only, it had been well over a month, and *Pandora was never given back like* the Perkins' said she would. Olivia called their home and went by their house late at night, and the Perkins wouldn't answer the door. Two months had gone by, then three, four, and five. *But no Anna.* Worry and Panic began to surface through Olivia's soul as the town people assumed she'd been killed. What had she done? Was Pandora dead? What had they done to her?" Olivia would see the Perkins' in the street, laughing and smiling for the public, but they refused to acknowledge her. After month six, Olivia began to get sick to her stomach in the realization of what may have happened with Pandora. As she sat in her living room sulking in her reality, she reached for the remote and turned on the television. The news popped on.

"In other news, it has been six months since the kidnapping of a fifteen-year-old girl here in Virginia Beach," A news reporter stood outside of Pandora's house. *"Police say Joanna Wilson, the daughter of Wells Fargo District Manager Joseph Wilson, was taken from the home right behind me in broad daylight. There have been searches throughout the state of Virginia, and rewards offered, yet police and search dogs have found nothing. It is believed that the young girl's body may have been dumped in the Ocean and possibly eaten by sea life. Search and Rescue teams have already begun to search for evidence. Police are asking anyone with details or clues that can lead the FBI to her whereabouts to please call."*

Regret washed over Olivia like the long, slow waves on the shallow beach. Each wave was icy cold, sending shivers down her spine. Whatever had happened to Pandora, it was because of *her*. Everyday Pandora didn't come home left a hole so big in Sophia's heart; she could barely breathe. She literally hung on to her soul by a thread. Oh, how Olivia longed to go back and choose a different path, but it was impossible. The remorse from it all ate her alive. Regret often came to her in quiet moments, such as when she was on her way to sleep, or when she stopped to take a lunch break at work. It would seep into the foreground of her mind and demand to be reexamined. Jumping up from the couch, Olivia walked into her powder room. Once there, she clutched her marble vanity and closed her eyes against the pale, stunned face she saw in the mirror. What had she done? Immediately, she burst into tears. Her stomach pitched and rolled like a ship in a storm. Had she eaten anything, she would've thrown up. She cried with more violence than any hurricane; as if the ferocity of it would bring Pandora back. Her soul felt tortured as the realization of what she'd done and who she'd become sunk in. She shivered, her skin breaking out in goosebumps, and her legs trembling. When Olivia's wracking sobs passed, she grabbed her cellphone and called the Perkins' once more. When they didn't answer, she slammed the phone down, grabbed her jacket and car keys and rushed out the front door. If the Perkins' wouldn't answer the door this time, *she would break it in…*

Pandora's memorial.
Quinn leaned against the pole of Pandora's memorial with her knees in her chest watching the local News Van drive off.
"Another day, another reporter," she glared, as it passed. "I wonder what conspiracy they're making up now. First, they said it was all a hoax. Then, you were supposedly a part of some secret government scandal. Now, they think you're dead. I just want them all to *go away*," Quinn fussed. "I'm so tired of this circus. You're not dead. The Anna I know is too stubborn to die before her time. You've got a whole life to live, and it's certainly not your time yet." Quinn missed her friend so much. They were like white on rice and tied at the hip for years. There wasn't a day that went by that the dynamic duo wasn't together. Now, it had been six months since Pandora mysteriously disappeared from her front

porch without so much as a trace. For Quinn, it felt like years. So much time had passed, and all that Quinn had left of her friend was fleeting memories. She held on to the sound of Pandora's voice and the touch of her skin. Every time Quinn thought about what could be happening to Pandora, her chest ached with fear. As she sat by her memorial dwelling on it some more, her face became wet with tears. They rolled silently onto her soft lips, salty and cold. For the life of her, Quinn couldn't fathom why God would give her such a good friend, only to snatch her away just like her father. Pandora was always the loudest voice in the room wherever she was. Her conversations were buoyant and intended to be heard. She spoke her honest truth, whether you wanted to hear it or not. She didn't care what Sophia said, and was unbothered by the big bad wolf that was Joseph Senior. On every subject, Pandora was opinionated. If you didn't agree with her, she wasn't angry; she just pitied you for not understanding. Quinn felt so free when she was around her. She could be herself, and she was happy. Now? Everything was wrong in her life. Beginning with her mother.

"*I hate my mom so much.* I want to run away and never come back but I don't have the guts to do it, and you're not here to talk me into it. She lied to my dad for so long. He found out through blood work by accident that he's not my dad at all." Quinn's eyes shifted to the side, glazed with a glossy layer of tears. As she blinked, they dripped from her eyelids and slid down her cheeks. She bit her lip tightly in an attempt to hide any sound that wanted to escape from her mouth. "Anna, he just walked away from me and didn't say goodbye. He disconnected his phone and disappeared. I don't understand, what did *I* do? I know he's mad at my mom, but I wasn't worth it to still love?" Her lower lip quivered as words slowly made their way out of her mouth.

"I'm so angry; I want to break something! And it didn't even phase my mom. You know, I walked in a few weeks ago, and I heard her sleeping with another man. And he sounded like a *woman*," she furrowed, angrily. "Some sissy, probably. I don't know what's happened to her; she's not herself anymore. Or maybe she was always like this and I'm just realizing it. Either way, I can't wait until you're back home. One day you and I, and Eden, we're gonna run this town. You're gonna be a lawyer, or a talk show host; or something that involves someone with a lot of mouth. I'm gonna be a Psychologist, and Eden's gonna be a nurse. We're gonna travel the world together, get married to our boyfriends, and have a ton of babies. *We won't be anything like our parents."*

Suddenly, Quinn saw her mother creeping toward her. Olivia looked around anxiously as if making sure no one saw her. Quinn sighed, irritated. She had no idea how her mother knew where she was, but she was ready to face whatever punishment she had coming her way for hanging the phone up on her. Just as Quinn stood up, Olivia turned the corner and walked up to the Perkins' front porch. That's when Quinn realized her mother hadn't even noticed her sitting there. Just as Quinn went to open her mouth and call for Olivia, Olivia began to bang on the Perkins' door. Before the Perkins' had a chance to answer, Olivia started banging on the window like the police. Quinn furrowed at the scene, rushing behind a nearby bush to get a better look. She saw Mr. Perkins crack open his front door in a huff. Quinn wasn't sure what was said, but when she saw her angry mother shove him out of the way and barricade herself into their home, she knew something wasn't right.

"Why is she shoving a handicapped man out of the way like that?" Quinn thought. Stealthily, Quinn began to approach the Perkins' house. She could hear Olivia's angry voice rambling on about something. Quinn stepped on to the porch, looked at the door handle and saw that the front door was cracked open. Mr. Perkins hadn't closed it all the way because he was too shocked that Olivia had nearly knocked his head off to get into the house. Quinn pushed the front door open ever so slightly, just enough to ease her tiny body inside.

"Get the hell out of my house before I call the police!" Mrs. Perkins fussed.

"*Call them.* Do us all a favor and let them come search this house for Sophia's little girl," Olivia yelled. She shoved both of the Perkins' out of the way and began to scream. "Anna!? Anna, are you in here? An-" With all the strength he had, Mr. Perkins dropped his cane, gripped Olivia up and shoved her into the wall.

"Have you lost your mind? I said get out of my house!"

"I'm not leaving until you give me Joanna. *We had a deal.* You told me you were taking her long enough for a fifty-thousand dollar monetary reward to be issued by the State. The reward is up to one hundred thousand dollars, and it's been six months! You still haven't given her back! You won't answer my phone calls, you won-"

"I haven't answered your phone calls because I don't have anything to say to you," Mr. Perkins scolded. "You did what we asked you to do. You helped us take the girl, and as a result, you got her mother, your little girlfriend, Sophia, back, and your secret kept."

"You lied to me! You got me involved in your little scandal, and it was all some sick lie. Where the hell is Anna? If you don't tell me, I will—"

A loud thud sounded at the front door, causing all three of them to snap their heads into the living room. Mrs. Perkins rushed into the living room and glanced at the front door. It was closed so she looked out the window but didn't see anyone.

"What was that?" Mr. Perkins walked into the living room. "Probably the wind closing the door." As Olivia continued with her threats, Quinn tiptoed up the rest of the stairs as quickly as she could. She was shaking, her heart was racing, and tears were flooding from her eyes like a river. As she listened to the conversation between her mother and the Perkins' from behind the couch, the wind slammed the front door shut and there was no way for her to get out without being seen. Without thinking, she ran up the Perkins' steps as quickly as humanly possible. Years ago, she remembered playing hide and seek with her friends. She decided to hide in a tree where she was certain she couldn't be found. After a half-hour of no one being able to discover her, Quinn dozed off and fell ten feet to the ground, landing on her back. The impact of her fall had knocked every whist of air from her lungs, and she lay on the ground struggling to inhale, to exhale— to do anything. That's how she felt in that very moment trying to remember how to breathe as she rushed into a bedroom, and slid under the bed. She couldn't believe what she'd heard. Quinn's blood ran cold, her fingers were jumping rhythmically, as if in a spasm. Her bowels suddenly churched and her stomach twisted into knots like she needed to vomit. Did she hear correctly? Were her mother and Sophia an item? The *Perkins'* were the ones who'd kidnapped Pandora, and her own *mother had* helped them? "No," she thought, shaking her head in denial. This has to be some sick joke. Quinn felt herself losing her mind. She could feel it unraveling, the threads of every happy memory of her mother shredding in disarray. She opened her mouth to cry, but not a sound would come out. Her head violently quivered as if there were a drill in the back of her skull. Tears ripped through her eyes. She couldn't take it anymore, and she couldn't hold in her scream. *Her own mother and the Perkins' had kidnapped her best friend.* Just as her horrifying scream began to surface, a pair of soft hands, grabbed her mouth.

"If you want to live, you need to suck it down and shut it up. *Now,*" a young female's whisper sounded in her ear. Quinn screamed as loud as she could, but the hands around her mouth muffled it.

"Shhh," The soothing warning begged a second time. She felt a hand rubbing her back, trying to calm her down. "I'm not gonna hurt you. I promise." Quinn turned her head to see a young girl that looked to be around her age under the bed next to her.

"If I take my hand from your mouth and you start screaming, my grandfather is going to come up here and kill you, and then he's gonna bury you under the house like the other girls. Do you want that?" Quinn's eyes widened as fear engulfed her conscious at the thought of being killed and buried under a house. She quickly shook her head no.

"Good." The girl moved her hand. "I'm Desiree. My family calls me Diamond. What's your name?"

"Quinn," Quinn's voice shook.

"Hi, Quinn. You look scared. Did he touch you yet?"

"Did who touch me?" Quinn raised her eyebrows.

"My grandfather. Did he snatch you from your parents?"

"No. No one snatched me. No one knows I'm here."

"What?" Desiree jerked her head back, "What the heck, how did you get in here?"

"My friend- my mom- I was just watching and-" Quinn paused to breathe in an attempt to calm her racing heart. Her emotions got the better of her and tears began to trickle down her face.

"Please calm down. I can't help you if I don't know what's happening."

Quinn took a deep breath. "My friend was kidnapped six months ago, and I just found out that Mr. and Mrs. Perkins took her. And my mother helped them. She's- I was- I heard her come in here and I snuck in to see what all the arguing was about, and I heard them talking. And then the front door shut and I got trapped in here, so I ran upstairs."

"Holy crap," Diamond peaked from under the bed to make sure she didn't hear anyone walking up the steps. "Did anyone see you?"

"I don't think so."

"Your friend. Is her name Anna?"

"Yes," Quinn's eyes grew big at the mention of Pandora's name.

"She's in the cellar. My grandpop has been raping her, and my grandmom has been beating her up. From what I hear when I'm around, I think she's still alive."

"Oh my God," Quinn winced, cupping her mouth to keep herself from screaming. "How did this happen? I don't understand. The Perkins' were always so nice to us."

"Nice? They're sick, twisted people. My grandfather has been molesting me since I was four years old. He's not my biological grandfather. The Perkins' don't have any children. His ex-wife had several. My mother is his stepdaughter, he was the only father she knew. They stayed close over the years, even though Mr. Perkins got married again. When I was born, she tried making me get close to him as well. My mother brings me over here every other weekend, and every other weekend I get violated. My mother doesn't know. He told me if I ever tell anyone, he'll kill me. If you think Mr. Perkins is bad, his wife is even more of a whack job. Both of them are completely nuts."

Desiree looked at her, "Your mother is a part of this too?"

"That's what I heard. I don't know what's going on, I just want to get my friend out of here."

"Girl, that cellar is blocked off by security cameras. My pop-pop practically lives down there with your friend. That is if she's even still alive."

"I've gotta get down there and find out."

"No. You've gotta find a way to get the heck out of here, or you'll be next. I wouldn't mess with crazy people."

"I have my phone. I can just call the police and tell them." Quinn reached in her pocket for her cellphone.

"No." Desiree grabbed her arm to stop her. "My grandfather used to be a Sherriff. Any call to a police station that raises a red flag on this house, someone will tip him off. They'll trace your number, find out who you are, and they will *kill* you." Diamond looked Quinn dead in her face. "I'm serious; just go."

"There's got to be a way to-"

"Diamond!" Mr. Perkins stomped up the stairs.

"Oh no," Diamond whispered in fear. Quinn's mouth parted open in fear. Her heart began to race.

"Diamond, where are you?" Mrs. Perkins called, following behind her husband. They both walked past the bedroom and into their master bedroom.

"Quinn. Get the hell out of here," Diamond warned. "If they catch you, you'll never leave."

"How do I get out?" Quinn asked.

"That window right there," Diamond pointed a finger in front of her. "As soon as you crawl from under the bed, there's a window in front of you. Unlock it and climb down the fire escape. It'll put you in the alley. From there, run like crazy and never look back."

"But what about my friend. How do I know if she's still alive?"

"I go home tomorrow. My mom comes to get me at seven o'clock. Do you live around here?"

"I live up the road."

"I can check the security camera to see if she's still alive. If she is, I'll leave the porch light on before I leave. My grandparents will probably turn it off, so you'll need to be lurking around near here exactly around seven."

"Okay."

"Diamond!" A pair of feet stood at the bedroom door. "Is that you under the bed?"

"Yes, pop-pop," Diamond responded quickly. She looked over at Quinn, "I'll distract them. Get out the window," She mouthed before climbing from under the bed.

"What are you doing down there?" Diamond got up from the bed looking afraid. "What's the matter?"

"I heard a bunch of screaming, and loud banging and I got nervous," Diamond lied.

"That was just some idiot from up the street. Nothing to be afraid of."

"I want a sandwich. Can you guys walk me downstairs to make one?' Diamond asked.

"You're sixteen years old; go make it yourself."

"I'm nervous. All that noise has me rattled. Can y'all just walk me down there to make sure no one got in here?"

"Desiree, there's no one-"

"Olivia just left out of here. Maybe we should double-check to make sure she's not trying to start any funny business," Mrs. Perkins eyed her husband. After thinking about it for a second, Mr. Perkins nodded.

"You're right." They both escorted Diamond down the steps. The second Quinn heard their voices in the distance, she slid from under the bed, rushed to the window, and practically jumped out of it. Her body trembled, and fear wracked every nerve she had, but she grabbed on to the fire escape ladder and crawled down as fast as she could. Despite the ambient evening temperature, Quinn's skin was icy. When her feet touched the ground, her adrenaline kicked in, and her legs exploded in a violent motion. She ran like a bat out of hell to her house. Sweat drenched her skin as her eyes throbbed, but she wouldn't stop until she made it home. Five minutes later, she ran up her front steps and darted into her house. The second she slammed the door, she let out a gut-wrenching scream, slamming herself against the door.

"Mannequin!" Olivia ran from the kitchen into the living room with a worried look on her face. "Baby, what's-

"They're raping her and beating her up, and it's all because of you!" Quinn screamed.

"What are you talking ab-"

"You psycho!!" she screamed deliriously, "I followed you into the Perkins' house and I heard everything."

Olivia froze. Her mind started to fail, like an engine that turns over and over, never kicking into action.

"That was you who slammed their front door," she spoke softly as if to confirm for herself. Before Olivia could open her mouth to speak another word, Quinn leaped at her mother's throat like an enraged panther.

"What did you do?!" Quinn screamed, knocking Olivia to the ground. Fires of fury and hatred were smoldering in her gray eyes.

"Mannequin, stop it," Olivia screamed back, gripping her daughter's hands to prevent Quinn from choking her.
"I hate you! You're gonna burn in hell."
"Quinn!" Olivia pushed her daughter off her and jumped up from the floor. "Let me explain, please," she began to cry.
"Just listen to me." Quinn was delirious. She screamed and hollered as her heart broke into a billion pieces. She ran for the door and raced outside. She wanted to run away but her legs gave away right there on the porch, and she fell to the ground crying. Olivia followed. She knelt down on the porch next to Quinn and begged her to listen, but Quinn didn't want to hear it. Her world turned into a blur, and so did all the sounds. The taste, the smell- everything was just gone. Tears burst forth like water from a dam. Emotional agony poured from every pore. Even at the top of the street, curtains were twitching as neighbors craned to locate the source of the screaming sobs. Olivia tried to hold her daughter back, to calm her, even as her own tears fell thick and fast. But in her hysteria, Quinn was too strong, too wild. At that moment, Olivia regretted everything. She thought Sophia's love was worth the cost of Pandora and worth lying to Steven. But to see her daughter so shattered from everything she'd done made her realize what was really important. Olivia lied to her daughter her entire life, and the residue of it all was now impossible to remove. Like an indelible stain on her cerebral cortex. She knelt down beside Quinn and cried with her.

Chapter 10

High School Graduation

It was the night before graduation, and the entire senior class of Salem High School flooded the local Pizzeria around the corner. Doughboys pizza was a popular hangout spot for much of the high school. It stayed open until midnight playing loud music, and most of the football team would go there after games to flirt with the girls and slurp on their famous root beer floats. Quinn and Pandora sat in a booth taking selfies with their cameras. Andre sat at a nearby table with his football team bopping to the music and tossing around a football. It was a sad, but joyous occasion. Almost everyone at the high school had grown up in the same neighborhood.

They played together as children, and now they were graduating high school. Some of them were off to college, some were going to trade school, and some had gotten left behind but still came to celebrate with their friends. Andre had a full-ride scholarship to Clemson University for football. He wanted to go but didn't want to go without Bruce. Andre was the football star he was because he played alongside his best friend. They were a duo, and he refused to play with anyone else. Bruce had gotten the same scholarship, but after Pandora's kidnapping, things changed for him. Her abduction took an emotional toll on him that nearly caused him to drop out of school. He was cut from the football team after he stopped showing up to practice, and he rejected his scholarship from Clemson.

There was no way he'd travel that far without knowing where the love of his life was, or what had happened to her and their unborn baby. He wouldn't have been happy, and he would've never been able to live with himself. After his mother and father freaked out about his decision, Bruce decided to attend Virginia State. When Pandora was found, Bruce was excited, but Pandora wasn't the same. *She'd changed.*

Pandora didn't want anything to do with Bruce. She was emotionally damaged and angry toward everyone. Bruce seemed to get the bulk of it. He tried talking to her, but she wouldn't listen. She didn't want Bruce touching her, telling her he loved her or coming over to her house. She was short-fused with a nasty, evil, attitude. She was rebellious and hateful and even went so far as to taking one of Bruce's teammates to the prom just to piss him off. The love they had was *no more*. The only loyalty Pandora had left was to Miss Ruby, Quinn, and Eden. Sitting in the booth, Quinn and Pandora stared at the selfie they'd just taken. Pandora wrapped an arm around Quinn's neck and laughed, lifting her camera for an encore photo. Quinn reminisced for a second, allowing the happiness she felt to soak into her bones. After nine months of hell, she and Pandora now smiled and laughed with ease. They talked excitedly about movies and the latest gossip. They drank their root beer floats and reminisced on their time in high school. For the first time in forever, Quinn's mind and body were relaxed. She stared at Pandora in awe as happiness overtook her. Pandora had gone through so much, and Quinn was elated she was still alive. She didn't know what it was about Pandora, but she felt so connected to her and so loyal to their friendship; there was no way she could ever see herself living without her. The night after Quinn escaped from the Perkins' and confronted her mother; her life had drastically changed. Quinn went from a spoiled little rich girl dating the star football player, headed to college, to a scared teenager in a horror film, carrying a secret she couldn't tell anyone. Every time Quinn would look at Olivia she grew disgusted and felt like she would throw up. Olivia explained everything to Quinn. She explained who Wilson was, and how she ended up with Steven. She explained who Big Joe was and how Sophia ended up with him. It all sounded like one sick twisted mess to Quinn. She watched in utter disbelief as her mother spilled the beans on her love life and all the dirt her and Sophia had done that had led to unwanted children. Quinn looked at her mother differently after that. Olivia wasn't at all the pretty eyed, good-spirited, graceful doctor that Virginia Beach knew and loved. She was evil with a conniving, deceitful persona. She was the devil in a lab coat with a stethoscope around her neck. And Quinn hated her. She had no respect for her as her mother or as a human being. After becoming fatherless, and now knowing what she knew about her mother, Quinn felt like her entire life had been a lie. Olivia warned Quinn never to speak a word of it to anyone.

"The damage is done. While I would love to go back and change it, I can't. If Pandora is still alive, and you go running to the police, they'll kill her. They will kill her. Then, they will arrest me and you'll be taken from me and sent into foster care. College is out of the question. Andre is out of the question. Whatever life you could potentially have would be out of the Question," Olivia cried. Quinn vowed not to utter a word, but it had nothing to do with *Olivia's* life potentially being ruined or her own. Quinn would've risked it all to keep Pandora safe. She vowed never to speak a word because when she walked to the park across the street from the Perkins house later that night, she could see Diamond walking out to her mother's car. Before she walked off the porch, *Diamond had cut the porch light on.*" In that sweet moment of victory, a relief valve went off in Quinn's mind.

Pandora was alive. She may have been raped, beat up, and tortured, but she was *alive.* If it cost Quinn her life, she was going to get her out. Over the next three months, Quinn risked everything to help Pandora. She informally moved into Miss Ruby's house. Olivia let her go, assuming Quinn could no longer stomach the sight of her. While that was true, it wasn't the reason. Miss Ruby lived up the street from the Perkins home, and two blocks over from Diamond. The night Diamond went back home with her mother, Quinn followed closely behind on her bicycle, careful not to be seen. When Diamond's car approached her driveway, Diamond's mother had gotten out to rush inside to the bathroom. Just as Diamond got out of her car, Quinn stood on the sidewalk in front of her.

"Quinn?" Diamond's eyes widened. "What are you doing here?" Fear filled Quinn's eyes as she spoke softly.

"I need your help."

"I helped you. I let you know your friend was still alive. I don't wanna get involved anymore and neither should you. Both of us will end up dead."

"What is happening to my friend isn't right. What's happening to *you is* not right," Quinn reached out and touched Diamond's hand. "You don't have to be molested by him every weekend. You don't have to live like this, and you don't have to fear for your life if you get away and save yourself."

"This is all I know," Diamond took her hand back and lowered her eyes. "I'm used to it, and I'm numb to it. It's better than fighting him."

"Please, let me help you," Quinn stared into her eyes. "Work with me. We can get Anna out, we can get you out, and we can get them put away forever."

Diamond looked at Quinn and thought for a while. She'd been raped since she was a little girl. She didn't like it but she was so afraid, she'd grown accustomed to the abuse. She didn't know any other way except violation. But something in Quinn's eyes told Diamond there was indeed another way. Another way that meant her body belonged to *her,* and she wouldn't have to sleep with anyone if she didn't want to. Another way that meant she could be free to be in a real relationship and eventually make love to someone she loved. Someone that wasn't her grandfather.

"Okay," Diamond agreed. "I'll help. But we have to act fast. My grandfather is obsessed with Anna. Every day he comes home he just sits in the cellar for hours with her. I think he got her pregnant a few times, but my grandmother beat the babies out of her."

Quinn gasped, nearly losing her balance. "My grandmom is super jealous and doesn't like it at all. She's planning a scholarship event in Anna's name with the high school. It's supposed to happen at the end of the summer just before senior year starts. After the meeting, she's gonna kill her."

Quinn felt a discomfort in her chest, and an anxious feeling surfaced through her brain as if she'd drank too much caffeine. Suddenly, she couldn't breathe. She felt as if someone were choking her. Her heart was racing, and all she wanted to do was curl into a ball and wait for someone to save Pandora. But no one would. No one was there. No one knew. *Except her*. The little girl who was constantly warned to sit still and look pretty would have to face her fears to save her best friend. Quinn was absolutely horrified at the thought of going through this alone. Part of her wanted to tell an adult, or her friends, or even Andre. Someone that could help her. But she couldn't. They'd mess everything up. If she wanted to help Pandora, she'd have to do it alone. Over the next three months, Quinn faced her fears and worked silently with Diamond. She stayed up endless nights trying to think of the right plan to save them. Each day, she treaded lightly and still acted normal. She stayed with Ruby and ended her day sitting by Pandora's memorial as she'd always done. A few days before the scholarship meeting, Quinn sat in the Doughboys Pizza Shop in complete and utter disarray. It had been three months since she found out Pandora was trapped in the Perkins' dungeon, and she couldn't for the life of her, figure out a way to get her out safely. She was running out of time, and if she didn't think quickly, Pandora would be dead. As her thoughts wandered, a young guy that looked to be in his thirties walked into Doughboys, laughing. Behind him was Mr. Perkins.

"Hey guys," the young man yelled to his friends who sat at the back table. "Look who it is! Old man Perkins." The other four guys stopped their conversation and looked. Immediately, they jumped up and rushed over to see Mr. Perkins.

"Hey Sherriff Perkins, it's been what, fifteen years now?" one of the guys said.

"It's been a long time, fellas. It's nice to see you again. Did you all try rejoining the police academy?"

"Heck no. Not after having you as a teacher. We all failed."

"Come over here and sit with us. Have a drink." Another guy asked.

"Oh no, I can't. I have narcolepsy. My medication is pretty much sensitive to every kind of pain killer and alcoholic drink around. I'd end up sleeping for days mixing the two."

"Oh come on Sherriff, just one drink. It won't kill you."

"I'm only here to grab a root beer float for my wife. How about we meet up on Thursday around five and we can catch up? But no drinking," he laughed. "You can buy me a seltzer water."

"It's a deal, man!"

Quinn watched them walk away, and an idea lit up in her mind like a light bulb. She wasn't sure if it would work, but she was out of options at this point and needed to try something. When Thursday approached, Quinn waited in Doughboys for Mr. Perkins to Arrive. She looked up narcolepsy medication and asked her mother what kind of drugs interacted with it. She told Olivia she had a project for school and needed to know.

"MAOI inhibitors interact dangerously with narcolepsy. Some of the more common ones are drugs used for ADHD, and Ativan, which is used for Anxiety. The Ativan is probably the least dangerous. It won't typically kill you, but for narcoleptic patients, it'd make them extremely drowsy to the point where they'd sleep a lot." *Ativan it was.* Quinn stole money from her mother's purse to pay two known thieves she knew from her class to break into Mr. Burton's pharmacy and steal a bottle of Ativan. They did it with ease and without getting caught. Quinn took three pills and placed it in the seltzer water she ordered. Just as she stirred it up and waited for it to dissolve, Mr. Perkins walked into Doughboys with his student.

"You take a seat, I'll grab our drinks."

Mr. Perkins sat down at the table as the guy walked up to the counter next to Quinn and ordered a root beer float for himself, and a seltzer water for Mr. Perkins. He paid for the bill in cash and the cashier told him his number would be called shortly. The guy nodded and quickly got distracted by his other buddies walking into the store. Two minutes later the cashier returned with their drinks. Just as she went to call him over the loudspeaker, Quinn intervened.

"My brother's drinks are ready? I'll take them over," she smiled.

"No problem," The waiter responded, handing the tray of drinks to Quinn. Quinn placed her spiked seltzer water on the tray and took the other one. Walking over to the guy, she tapped him.

"Here you go. The cashier told me to give these to you."

"Oh thank you, great. I'm sorry. I didn't hear anyone calling my number," he took the tray from Quinn.

"No problem. Enjoy."

That was the last chance Quinn had at a foolproof plan. She watched the guy walk to the table with Mr. Perkins and hand him his water. To her surprise, it worked beautifully. Mr. Perkins gulped the entire thing down. Forty-five minutes later the scholarship meeting was just getting ready to start, and people were beginning to collect outside to take their seats. Diamond found her way to Quinn and passed on that she overheard her grandfather talking to himself in the bathroom. He rambled on about molesting Pandora one last time before the meeting ended, and Mrs. Perkins killed her. Quinn felt her stomach turning knots. Part of her wanted to run into the Perkins home, causing a scene along the way that would make everyone else follow so they could find Pandora.

"*Don't do that*. You made it this far. We have to keep going. My grandfather, at some point, is going to pass out- or die from all that medication you gave him. He nearly fell out of the bathroom a few minutes ago," Diamond said. "If you can keep my grandmom occupied, I can go in and unlock the cellar door and get Anna to come out."

"Does she know who you are?" Quinn asked.

"No," Diamond replied with a somber glow. "I've seen her on the cameras. She's never met me, so there's a slight chance she may not trust me."

"We can give it a shot. If that doesn't work, we can try something else."

Quinn motioned for Mrs. Perkins to come over and talk to her while Diamond slowly made her way toward her grandparent's house. Just as she was about fifteen feet away from the front porch, the Perkins' front door burst open, and Pandora sprung forth like a zombie back to life. It was one of the best days of Quinn's life. She'd done it. *The girl who grew up feeling like all she had to offer was her beauty, had saved her best friend's life and* not just her life, but she also saved Diamond. As the Perkins' were being taken away in handcuffs, Diamond's mother and Father looked terrified as they clutched their daughter. Diamond's mother had trusted her stepfather and had no idea what he'd been doing to little girls all these years. As they rushed Diamond into their car to swarm her away from the growing media, Diamond and Quinn locked eyes. She mouthed Quinn a *Thank you*. Quinn smiled back. *Freedom*. Pandora had a good senior year of high school, despite her set back. Quinn wanted to tell her everything that happened, but Pandora had gone through enough, and it just wasn't worth it. As the school year went on, Pandora left her home and went to live with Ruby.

Ruby saw to it that Pandora excelled in her school work, and helped her get into Virginia State. Things had begun to return to normal. Well, as normal as life could get considering the circumstance. Sophia tried to continue her relationship with Olivia. She even offered to leave her husband so they could be one big family. But Olivia pushed back. She couldn't stomach being in an open relationship with Sophia more than she could stomach walking around as if everything were okay. Guilt ate away at her too badly, and she just wanted to be left alone. She took on more hours at the hospital, and Quinn stayed cooped up under Ruby. The mother/daughter duo barely saw each other anymore, and both of them were relieved. Olivia lingered in the background of her daughter's life and saw how much she'd grown during senior year. Quinn was a straight-A student, she'd gotten a full scholarship to Virginia State, and she'd be attending there with the love of her life.

"I feel so bad for him," Quinn glanced over at Bruce. He sat by himself and played with his phone, periodically glancing up at the football team. He missed his friends and wished he hadn't given up on football for a girl who ended up hating him.

"Don't. We didn't tell him to quit football. He did that on his own," Pandora replied.

"He did it for you, Anna, and now he's come out of everything empty-handed."

"I guess that's why they tell you not to put all your eggs in one basket," Pandora responded coldly. "I'm excited to be graduating tomorrow. Can you believe we made it?"

"It's been a journey," Quinn agreed, "I'm glad to be getting away from this crazy, lunatic town. I hear Virginia State has a lot to offer."

"Ditto. Have you decided what you want to major in? I wanted to do music, but Miss. Ruby is making me do accounting."

"Music? I didn't know you could sing?" Quinn chuckled.

"I can't. It just seems easier than accounting," Pandora giggled.

"I think I'm gonna do psychology. This Advanced Placement psych class I've been taking all year is interesting. I can definitely see myself being a therapist one day."

"Really?" Pandora looked shocked. "I didn't know you enjoyed helping people. You usually sit back and let everyone else shine."

"I had a revelation this year," Quinn smirked, containing her secret. "It forced me to stop hiding, be brave, and reach out to those in need." Saving Pandora and Diamond had given Quinn a new lease on life. She felt like she'd done something meaningful, and she felt so empowered by it, she wanted to continue it for the rest of her life. She always found psychology interesting, but after that fiasco, she was sure of it.

"That's pretty cool. Well, maybe you can start with *Bruce over* there who looks like he wants to go into the bathroom and hang himself," Pandora laughed. Quinn huffed and shook her head at Pandora. Hopefully, she and Bruce would find their way back to each other soon.

"Hello Ladies," A familiar, sweet voice approached their table. Quinn and Pandora looked up to see Olivia standing there with a faint smile. Dressed in her usual lab coat and stethoscope, she gazed at both of the girls.

"Hi, Mrs. Olivia, Pandora's face lit up. She immediately got up to hug her.

"Hi sweetheart," Olivia wrapped Pandora in her arms and rubbed her back as her eyes slid closed. "Oh my goodness, I'm so glad you're alive and doing well. I prayed for you every day." Quinn almost jumped across the table after her mother told that bald-faced lie.

"Thank you so much," Pandora smiled, "Would you like to eat with us?"

"I don't think so," Quinn got up from the booth to face her mother. She tried her best to appear pleasant, but her anger was beginning to seep through the cracks of her emotions. "We're actually getting ready to leave."

"What? Why? We just got here," Pandora replied, confused.

"It's alright," Olivia smiled, "I'm actually on my way to work. I just wanted to come by and tell you ladies how proud I am of you. And I wanted to speak to my daughter if that's okay," her eyes lifted to meet Quinn's.

"I'm a little busy. Can we talk later?" Quinn bit, irritated.

"I have to work until five a.m, so I'm sure you'll be sleeping when my *later is* available. It'll really only take a few minutes," Olivia insisted.

"Well, I don't-"

"Quinn, what's up with you?" Pandora winced, "has my mouth started to rub off on your good girl persona?" she laughed, "talk to your mother. I'm gonna go over here and bother your boyfriend and the rest of the football players."

"Fine," Quinn folded her arms and watched Pandora walk away. She so badly wanted to follow her.

"Mannequin, can we talk?" Olivia sat at the table. "Have a seat." Quinn slumped herself in the booth and looked the other way. "Look at me," Olivia reached across the table and clutched her daughter's hands. "Please?" Quinn snatched her hands away and turned to face the woman she'd known all her life as "*mom*". Olivia was still one of the most beautiful women to ever grace the city of Virginia Beach. Even as she sat in Doughboys, a few high school boys glanced her way. Quinn stared lifelessly at the gray eyes she once thought were beautiful. Looking at them now, Quinn couldn't find one trace of the vibrancy they once held, no trace of the mother she once knew. Olivia had fooled the world with that refined look of innocence she possessed. She'd pulled the wool over Quinn's eyes for years. Olivia hid her drama beneath her pretty until one day Quinn glimpsed the curtains and the stage lights and spotted the repetition of Olivia's schemes. She wasn't the sheep everyone thought she was. *She was a wolf.*

"Listen, I know you hate me for everything that's happened," Olivia pursed, "I hate myself for it all. I've watched you throughout senior year and saw you grow into a young woman right before my eyes. I'm excited to hear you've been accepted into my alma mater," she choked down a cry as her eyes watered. "Sophia told me. I didn't even know you applied."

"Was I supposed to tell you?" Quinn tilted her head, "Were we supposed to have this beautiful mother-daughter bond where I could invite you into my future?"

"I could've at least helped you fill out a financial aid form."

"I didn't need your information," Quinn rebutted, "I filed as an independent. Thankfully I was awarded a scholarship, but even if I wasn't, I didn't want your name on *anything*. You're a monster, and I will *never forgive* you for what you've done. You tried to ruin *my life*, but God covered me." A tear fell from Quinn's eye. "You tried to ruin Anna's life, you ruined Steven's life, and you ruined Sophia's life. All in the name of *selfishness*; so y*ou* could be happy." Quinn raised her root beer glass. "Well, cheers to you. You got what you wanted. Anna hates her mother and lives with Miss. Ruby. I'm not in the house anymore, and Joseph is already in College. Big Joe is never home because he's out cheating on Sophia. That leaves you and Sophia to yourselves, left to live in your own sick twisted perversion for the rest of your miserable lives," she sneered.

"I told Sophia everything," Olivia shot back quickly. "I never mentioned that you found out, but I did confess what I did. She hates me. She never wants to see me again, and if she was bold enough, she'd call the authorities and make them lock me up along with the Perkins'," she sniffed, reaching for a tissue as she wiped her face.

"So what do you want from me?" Quinn raised an eyebrow. "Pity?"

"No," she shook her head softly. "I don't want pity. I want you to learn from my mistakes. Unfortunately, I failed at showing you the right way to live. I want you to observe my life and use it as a tool for the way not to live," her face turned bright red as the stain of guilt overtook her. "A pretty *face can hide so much.* You've been blessed with beauty. Don't hide behind it. Live in your truth, and whomever you tell the world you are, *be that.* Don't hide behind secrets; don't hide behind those pretty eyes. You love hard, and you be honest. I'm so sorry that I failed. I have to live with that every day of my life, but I don't want you to do that," her voice shook. "You are a good person. You are a loyal person, and you're a good friend. You and Andre are gonna get married someday. I look at you two, and I see how much you both are meant for one another. You and Anna and Eden, you guys are gonna be friends for the rest of your lives. *Always be true to them.* Keep them close," Quinn's lip trembled as she listened to her mother speak. She hated that they were broken, and she hated that they couldn't be fixed. Life as Quinn knew it had been ripped from under her. She had her best friend back, but she lost everything else.

"*You did this*. You ruined my life. It wasn't supposed to be this way. I was supposed to graduate, go to college, get married, have children, and live happily ever after. You and Dad read me fairytales growing up, and you made me believe in happy endings and good people. You made me believe in a mother's unconditional love and a father's affection. And it was all *lies*." Quinn shook her head and folded her arms. "I don't want to *ever* see you again. I don't want to see your proud face when I go off to college. If I ever get married, I don't want you at my wedding, and if I ever have children, you'll never see them. You took everything from me, and now I have to rebuild it. I'm broken and confused because of *you*," she forced the words out and wiped her face as more tears flooded.

"I'm sorry. That's all I can offer you," her mother sighed. Olivia cast her gaze onto her daughter, and her eyes darkened. The guilt she felt vibrated through her chest and into her brain. She'd gone to church the previous Sunday and cried her eyes out at the alter. But it didn't matter how much she begged God for mercy and forgiveness; she felt like she was beyond redemption or rebirth. Olivia felt like the damage she'd done would forever be a scar over her heart. "I pulled you into my arms with one hand, and I pushed you away with the other," her voice sounded more pained than anything. "But I want to leave you with this, and then I'm gonna go to work. With time, *everything heals*. Your body heals. Your heart heals. The mind heals. Wounds heal. Your soul repairs itself. Your happiness will find its way back. One day, you'll come back from this, and when you do, you remember my life. Remember that in all of my flaws, your mother loved you," she wiped her flustered face and slid out of the booth. "I'm not even gonna bother to come to your graduation because I know I'm not welcome." Olivia faced her daughter. "I wish you the best of *everything that* life has to offer." Reaching down, she softly kissed her daughter on the forehead. "Congratulations." Quinn jumped up from the table and rushed into the nearest bathroom to cry her eyes out. Olivia painfully watched her daughter walk away for the last time and then turned around and walked out of the pizzeria. She went to work that night, and she went home that next morning. At ten a.m, Dr. Olivia Michelle Gray walked into her basement and grabbed her ex-husband's shotgun from the shelf.

"Lord, watch over my baby. Cover her heart and her mind. Protect her from this sick, dying, evil world. Give her good measure in the form of genuine love from her friends, and from the man you see fit to marry her. She's a diamond in the rough. Make her name *great*, and at some point in her life, let her remember that in spite of my selfishness, I loved her to the moon and back." Pulling the trigger, she sent a bullet straight through her head.

Chapter 11

"A queen never leaves her throne to address a peasant throwing stones."

"I don't understand," Pandora held up a tiny onesie from the gift bag that was given to her by a coworker, "how can clothing be organic?"

"Maybe it's the cotton they use," Eden replied, confused.

"Or the dyeing process. Welcome to the world of millennium parenting. Don't be surprised if you see a gluten-free sign over a bag of socks," Quinn laughed. Herself, Eden, and Pandora shared a sofa in the lounging area at Olives, a martini bar and restaurant. It was Pandora's last day of work before her maternity leave, and Eden requested they all celebrate that evening at the newly opened restaurant, owned by one of her salon client's sons. Some of Pandora's co-workers had stopped by the lounge to give her a few gifts in celebration of her upcoming big day.

"That's ridiculous," Pandora placed the onesie back into the bag and closed it. "This is a really nice hangout spot. Who do you know that owns this place?"

"A good friend of my mother's that still comes to the Salon to get her hair done. Her son is the owner here, and she's been raving about this place since it opened. I researched it and saw some really good reviews so I thought we'd check it out."

"It's super nice," Quinn nodded, giving her seal of approval.

"Hi, Eden," A guy that looked to be in his late twenties approached the lounge area.

"Oh shoot, here he is. This is the son I was just talking to you about," Eden stood up and smiled. "Hey, Stephan."

"Hey ladies," The five foot eleven, butter almond owner with dark eyes and a boyishly handsome face, smiled back. "Welcome to Olives."

"Hello *Stephan*," Pandora and Quinn replied in unison with a grin. Pandora nudged Eden and pursed her lips as Quinn began to ask questions.

"This is a really nice place. How old are you? You look a little young to own a lounge."

"I'm good with money," Stephan blushed, "I'm twenty-eight."

"Guys, don't embarrass me," Eden threatened between her teeth.

"What a coincidence. *Eden* is twenty-eight," Pandora clapped her hands together.

"Right. I think his fiancée is twenty-eight as well," Eden intervened quickly. "Is she here so we can introduce her to my inquiring minded girlfriends?" Stephan laughed.

"She was," he looked around, "she may have stepped out to speak with the bouncers. I'll definitely bring her around for you guys to meet when I run into her again. In the meantime, enjoy the place. All the drinks," he noticed Pandora's pregnant belly, "and juice, are on the house tonight. Enjoy ladies."

"We certainly will," Quinn smiled as he walked away.

"I like him. He's cute," Pandora nodded.

"You know, y'all just can't just go offering me up to the highest bidder without first finding out if they're taken."

"You said he had a *fiancée*. He's not taken yet," Pandora confirmed.

"Anna," Quinn laughed. "He was cute, Eden. *And* an entrepreneur, which means he's responsible."

"He's cute," Eden agreed. "But his feet aren't big enough for me."

"Oh, hell." Pandora looked to see if she could catch a glimpse of his foot size before he was out of sight. "You're full of crap. His feet aren't small."

"He looks like an even size eleven," Eden replied. "I need a man with a thirteen." Quinn quickly covered her ears.

"I am not listening to this. You are a baby."

"Quinn, I'm almost thirty years old. I'm grown. At some point, you'll have to accept it," Eden chuckled.

"Nope. You are the baby. You've never had a boyfriend, and you're still a virgin. That's my story, and I'm sticking to it."

"I agree," Pandora intervened. "And besides, when you fall in love it's not the size of the boat that makes a difference. Shoot, the Titanic wasn't even reliable. At the end of the day, they used a tugboat to save their behinds." All three of them shared a laugh.

"Maybe I'll find the love you guys have. *Someday*. But I'll never get married again, ever," Eden sneered.

"I promised myself the same thing," Pandora rebutted. "All of that will go out the window when you find the man *you're* meant to marry."

"I was engaged once for like twenty minutes my

senior year of high school, and I was married for a couple of months to Travis. That does it for me. No more marriage, ever. My game face is on. I mean it."

"Yeah, yeah. You talk tough, but on the inside, you're a marshmallow." Quinn wrapped an arm around her and squeezed.

"I believed in love because of you and Andre," Eden said. "And after hearing that he filed for divorce and then took another woman out on a date?" Eden winced, "You guys were my fairytale. If you can't make it; there's no hope for any of us."

"My sentiments exactly," Pandora shook her head. "I mean, I totally get the separation thing. It was warranted from a lack of communication. But divorce? Shouldn't both parties get a vote? Andre didn't mention it to you or try to negotiate anything. He just handed you *papers*."

"He did." Quinn picked up Eden's martini glass and took a big gulp." Eden and Pandora watched in surprise.

"You drink?"

"I am tonight. As long as you keep reminding me of my shattered marriage that I'm so eloquently trying to forget."

"We're sorry," Pandora felt bad.

"It's okay. At some point, I'll deal with it all. I'm just not ready yet."

"Well, I have something better than liquor that might help," Eden checked her watch and then stared at the door. Her eyes lit up with a devious grin when a tall, dark and handsome man walked through.

"What is it?" Quinn lifted her glass of cranberry juice off the table.

"Another woman at the salon has a twin brother, Damon. He just walked in," Eden smirked, pointing at the door. "He's sexy and single. And you're sexy and somewhat single. So I set you both up on a not so blind date." Quinn spit her juice out of her mouth and choked.

"You did what?" Pandora watched the man at the door looking around for Eden, as she patted Quinn's back.

"Come on Quinn," Eden's eyes pleaded. "It's just drinks. You need *some* type of distraction. You don't have to go home with the guy, but it would be nice to get out around some male company to take your depressed mind off of Andre."

"Eden, have you lost *all* of your mind?" Quinn stared at Eden like she had five heads.

"No. I haven't. But you will if you don't get it together. He's a nice guy."

"I don't care if he was Jesus Christ," Quinn jerked her head back, "I'm a public figure. I can't be seen with another man that's not my husband."

"Well you're husband certainly doesn't mind being seen in public with a woman that's not his wife. Look." Pandora nudged her head to the far left. Eden and Quinn turned to see Andre in the secluded restaurant area of the lounge having dinner with the same woman from the photo Quinn's patient had sent her just weeks before. Quinn's heart almost stopped. Eden gasped. If Quinn suffered from anxiety, she'd have gone into a full-blown attack.

"This is ridiculous," Pandora sneered, "And downright disrespectful. He doesn't even look happy with her. What's his deal?"

"One of his friends probably told him to do the same thing I'm telling Quinn to do," Eden rolled her eyes at the woman. "I can't believe his nerve." Before anyone could say anything else, Pandora reached into her purse and pulled out a penny. Rearing her arm back, she tossed it across the restaurant, hitting the woman right in the side of the face. The woman jumped back, not knowing what hit her. Andre was too busy staring at the game on the television to notice. Quinn, Pandora, and Eden quickly shifted in another direction.

"*Anna*," Eden whispered, "Why would you *do* that?"

"Jesus Christ, Pandora," Quinn stood up. "I'm leaving."

"Quinn," Pandora stood up, "That's *your* husband. He's been *yours* since middle school, and he's supposed to be *yours* until death do you part. He's also supposed to forsake all others. Others meaning that *skank* he's with. I don't know what's going on, but something isn't right. Andre would never ask you for a divorce. He'd die mad at you but he'd never just let you go like that. And the same with you," she winced. "Since when are you okay with this?"

"I'm not okay with it, Anna. If the man doesn't want me, he doesn't wan-"

"He *wants* you. He loves you. He's lost without you. Look at him sitting over there listening to her talk. He looks like he wants to blow his brains out." All three of them turned around. Quinn looked at Andre. As usual, she lost her breath at the sight of him, which reignited her faded irritation. Why did he have that effect on her? When was she going to become immune? Although her friends were a bit fanatical, there was some truth in their statement. Andre looked *miserable*. Suddenly, the flustered woman got up from the table and began walking their way.

"Uh oh," Eden bit.

"Great," Quinn sighed, "I don't feel like any trouble tonight. It's bad enough I-"

"Mannequin Bentley. Stop being so *weak*. Let her bring her behind over here and say something smart so we can snatch that cheap-looking pocketbook she's carrying and throw it in *the trash.*" Eden looked at the woman's purse and burst into laughter. Quinn lowered her head and fused her lips together trying not to laugh. "Get your husband. Open the line of communication and put an end to this madness. We can do things *that* way. Or, if this dollar store purse carrying bimbo comes any closer, I can shoot her, and we'll save-"

"No!" Quinn and Eden protested.

"God, please. *No*. Keep your gun in your-"

"Well hello, ladies. I think one of you lost your penny." The woman approached them. Although she addressed everyone, she studied Quinn, never taking her eyes off her. The woman was even more gorgeous in person than she was in the photo her client sent. She was tall and slender, with big dark eyes and a cascade of straight brown hair. Her lips were lush and red, her cheekbones high and sculpted. Her dress was modestly sexy and contrasted beautifully with her almond skin. She looked like an exotic supermodel.

"My apologies. I was reaching for change to tip the waiter, and my hand slipped," Pandora gave a fake smile.

"I'm sure," The woman returned the fake smile and looked at Quinn. "It's nice to finally meet you, Mannequin. I'm Grace," she stuck out her hand. Quinn considered taking her hand and shoving it down her throat until she choked to death, but the modesty in her could never be that petty. Instead, she smiled and shook Grace's hand.

"It's a pleasure," Quinn replied.

"Listen, I just wanted to clear the air. Andre and I have been seeing one another off and on for a few months now. I'm not trying to step on your toes. He hasn't mentioned you, and I'm not sure what's going on between you two. I found out from a friend that you two were separated. I remembered your face from TV. I used to always watch you two on the word channel on Sunday mornings. I just wanted to let you know that I'm sorry about your recent struggles and that whenever you guys are fully divorced, I plan to get serious with Andre." Eden and Pandora jerked their heads back in disbelief at her nerve.

"Is that so," Quinn replied sweetly. Although her demeanor was calm, her eyes were like knives. She calmly glared at the woman like she could slice her throat.

"It is," Grace nodded. "He's a good man. He's a powerful man, and he's an amazing pastor."

"Anything else you'd like to tell me about *my* husband?"

"You mean soon to be *ex*-husband? No. That's it. I'm coming to you as a woman and just wanted to make sure we wouldn't have any," she glanced at Pandora and Eden, "further problems?" Quinn stared at the woman and then averted her gaze toward Andre. Grace was beautiful, but Quinn was irreplaceable. Andre loved Quinn for her modesty, her poise, and her demeanor. Quinn was graceful and respectful. This woman appeared mouthy and had a *serious* attitude that Andre would never deal with. It became evident the more Grace talked that he wasn't interested in this woman. Quinn had no idea why he chose to be seen in public with her, but this fiasco had gone a little too far. Pandora was right. Andre was *her* man. She allowed her pride to get in the way for over six months. This charade and distance between them had gone on too long. It was time to open the line of communication and save her marriage. But did he still love her? If she reached out, would he still care? *There was only one way to find out.*

"Problems?" Eden looked at the woman in disgust, "The only problem is your-"

Quinn lifted a hand to discourage Eden from finishing her sentence. "There will be no more problems. Thank you so much for being a woman," Quinn smiled.

"I respect that," Grace confirmed with a head nod. "I'm gonna get back to my soon to be man. You ladies have a wonderful evening." The woman turned and walked back to her seat. Quinn turned around to face Eden.

"Eden, where's that guy you brought in for me," She grinned mischievously. Eden and Pandora blinked in surprise. They glanced at Quinn, then the woman, and then back again before they finally understood what was getting ready to happen.

"Right over there at the bar," Eden's smile was infectious. Her hazel brown eyes crinkled at the corners and her mouth curved up, "I'll go get him."

Ten minutes later Quinn walked over to a secluded table, just shy of Andre and Grace. As she walked toward the table, Quinn wanted to pause and maybe bang her head against the wall. Why did she do this to herself? And why must she now go through antics to get her husband back? She hoped she still remembered *how* to date. After being with Andre for so long, being cordial with other men wasn't her strong suit. Damon stood up and smiled at her. He was about six feet tall with dark hair, dark eyes, and a crooked smile. He was tanned and fit, but not in a look-at-me kind of way. And he was staring at Quinn as if she had a monkey on her head. His gaze was steady. Quinn couldn't stand it anymore.

"You're staring at me," she said, trying to keep her voice as friendly as possible. "Is something wrong?" Damon's eyes widened, then he glanced away before returning his attention to her.

"No. Sorry. Jeez, I'm being an idiot. It's just…you. *Wow*. I saw you walking toward me, and I figured there had to be a mistake. Then I saw you approaching my table, and you are absolutely gorgeous…" He verbally stumbled to a stop, then cleared his throat. "Can we start over or do you want to leave?" His expression was both chagrined and hopeful. Quinn tried to remember the last time anyone had been so rattled by her looks. She knew she was beautiful, but considering the last six months, it was the last thing on her mind. She didn't feel beautiful at all. It felt good to be reminded. She smiled.

"We can start over."

"Good. I'll do my best not to be scary." He smiled. "It's nice to meet you, Mannequin."

"Apparently," Quinn laughed. The sound of her familiar laugh caused Andre to look up. All the color nearly drained from his face when he saw his wife sitting just a few feet away from him. *And with another man.* Quinn and Andre locked eyes and maintained eye contact, unable to look away. They felt drawn to one another, as if a rope bound their waist and they were slowly, inexorably pulling themselves closer. Blinking out of her semi daze, Quinn released him. Andre wasn't just beautiful; he was enthralling. She missed him. *She wanted him.* But she had a job to do first. Reverting her eyes back to her date, she and Damon began to talk and laugh. Andre's nostrils engulfed the delicate hint of Quinn's aura in the air, and he stared at his wife. Her face was just as pretty as the first day he saw her, her gray eyes twinkling with laughter and her teeth glistening as she smiled. It seemed as if so much time had passed, and the only thing Andre had left was the occasional fleeting memory. He'd lost the sound of her voice and the touch of her skin. His chest ached as he thought of what he lost. No one had ever replaced Quinn, and no one ever would.

"Are you alright, sweetheart?" Grace said, "You haven't touched your food."

"Fine," Andre focused back on Grace. He'd forgotten she was sitting there. He had no idea why he allowed one of the deacons at church to set him up with her. He knew they were trying to help him take his mind off Quinn, but it wasn't working. Grace was beautiful but other than that she was annoying.

"Try the red wine," she smiled, passing it to him. "A friend told me it was delicious." Andre took the glass into his hands. He tried not to pay attention to Damon and Quinn, but he couldn't help it. He couldn't see Damon's face, but he saw his hand move closer to Quinn's face. His eyes grew big and furious as he squeezed the glass. Damon took his finger and wiped the residue of salad dressing from Quinn's lips, and that was all it took. Andre burst like fireworks on the fourth of July. He squeezed the glass in his hand until it shattered to pieces. He stood straight up as wine spilled all over the table and himself.

"Oh my gosh, are you alright?" Grace looked concerned. Quinn looked at Andre and Damon turned around. Andre looked at him like an angry, trapped tiger ready to pounce.

"Oh man, are you alright?" Damon innocently stared back. He saw the shattered glass and the blood coming from the cut in Andre's hand. Grace looked back and saw Quinn. When she noticed her with another man, she knew exactly what was going on.

"She's with another man. She's *really* done for now," Grace thought with a smirk, immediately helping Andre clean up. She just knew Andre would fall apart and she would be there to pick up the pieces of him.

"I'm fine, thanks," Andre responded to Damon, keeping his gaze locked on Quinn.

Damon and Grace helped Andre clean up the shattered glass and juice as a waiter approached the table and assisted with the rest. Quinn and Damon talked and laughed about their careers and things that interested them for the next thirty minutes or so while Grace talked to Andre, who was too jealous and absorbed in Quinn to hear anything she said.

Eventually, Damon's phone rang, and he needed to cut the date short. He stood up, thanked Quinn for her time and asked if it was okay to exchange numbers. Respectfully, she took his number and offered to call *him* instead when she was ready. He agreed, they shared a hug, and he had left. Standing up, Quinn turned on her heels and strutted toward the bathroom of the restaurant, capturing her husband's gaze along the way. Her long lashes framed her eyes as she seductively scanned him up and down. Andre's focus immediately turned to stone. Their stares lasted a full second, enough for each to take in the face of the other. Nothing needed to be said. Millions of years of evolution had already taken care of the message. With just the right look of heat in her eyes, Quinn motioned for him to join her in the bathroom.

"I'm so sorry, Grace," Andre quickly stood up, "I have to go."

Grace looked at Andre and then turned to see what he was staring at. Her mouth opened when she saw Quinn prancing toward them. Grace stood up, embarrassed and angry."

"What is going on?" She fussed at Quinn, "We're trying to have dinner!"

"You've had your dinner, honey," Quinn graced pass them. "I plan on being dessert," Quinn disappeared into the bathroom. Andre followed her, nearly stumbling over his own two feet trying to get into the bathroom behind her. Grace stomped her foot and seethed in anger. She turned to her left to see if anyone had seen. Eden laughed senselessly while Pandora winked, flashing her adorable dimples as she waved goodbye. An angry Grace grabbed her purse and stormed out of Olives. The second the bathroom door was shut, Andre caught his wife by the waist, hauling her off her feet, directly into his chest. The air left Quinn's lungs in a rush, followed immediately by every bit of common sense she possessed. Even though the layers of clothing between them, Andre's biceps were like stone beneath her palms, his stomach, a hard slab of muscle against her own.

"I love you," He rasped. "I can't eat, or sleep, or think straight without you." Quinn melted into him as her body went lax. Tears slipped free and ran down her face.

"I love you, too. You have the power to hurt me like no one else can. And you did that. You asked me for a divorce, and then you took another woman on a date."

"She was just a distraction," he paused, tears flooding his eyes. "I thought you hated me. You wouldn't look at me, you were screaming at me. You seemed disgusted and turned off. Diamond-I-I felt like my past had pushed you too far away, so I gave you what I thought you wanted."

"Your past doesn't have the power to push me

away. Only you can do that."

"I didn't know what to do," Andre said, "I never wanted you to see me like this. I've *crawled* through the last month without you. I'm sorry." Tears tore from his eyes. "Can we fix it? I don't want to give you up," he kissed her. "I can make you want me again. Let me try," he begged.

"We can fix it," Quinn replied. She could feel the raging beat of his heart against her chest, proof that he wasn't just a hopeless ordeal conjured by her fevered imagination. *True love never died.* In spite of it all, it lived on. He went to speak, but Quinn sealed her lips over his and silenced him. Andre kissed her back like he could eat her alive…and he surely tried to.

He did things to her in that bathroom that had to be considered a sin, but since Quinn was probably on her way to hell for murder anyway, she figured she might as well enjoy the ride. They went back to Andre's apartment that night and spent the entire night talking, trying to find a way to fix what was broken. Andre promised Quinn he would never hurt her again and made the sweetest love to her over and over again until he was sure she believed him. The next morning, Andre gazed up and down his wife's beautiful body and crawled all over it for as long as she would let him. They barely made it through breakfast before the syrup became a part of foreplay and they were back at it again. *Finally,* the lover her heart had broken for, returned to her.

Chapter 12

"For we know all things work together for the good of them that love God, and who are called according to his purpose." –Romans 8:28

Quinn and Andre spent the next few days locked away in Andre's apartment trying to fix their broken marriage. There were secrets that needed to be revealed and truths that needed to be told. Both of them were committed to the task. In some moments they cried, other times they prayed, and others they sat still and said nothing. Everything was far from alright, but they knew time would heal all wounds. Leaning against the kitchen counter, Andre nuzzled Quinn against his chest. Quinn stroked down his neck and caressed his high cheekbones. She was soft, warm, and a reassurance that God did *all* things well.

"Are you up for a walk in the Park?" Andre asked softly.

"Maybe a little later," Quinn replied, taking a sip of her coffee.

"Mommy?" Quinn and Andre turned as Heaven walked into the kitchen.

She was tousled and still half-asleep. One hand held her battered, red stuffed toy, Betty the Dragon. The well-loved plush dragon was based on the popular series of children's books. Quinn took another sip of her coffee before setting it on the counter and leaning down to scoop up her daughter.

"Good morning sleepyhead," she planted kisses on her cheeks.

"Baby!" Andre held his arms out, excited. Heaven smiled and dropped Betty. Certainly, no dragon could compare to her daddy. She nearly leaped out of Quinn's arms to get to Andre. He wrapped his arms around her waist, while she settled hers around his neck, hanging on with her legs. Andre pretended to stagger as he lifted her. "You grew!" Heaven giggled at the familiar comment.

"I not grow," she told him.

"I think you did." He rebutted. Quinn walked over and kissed her fluffy cheeks again, breathing in the scent of her skin. Whatever went wrong in their day, Heaven was always right. She was the glue that kept Quinn and Andre moving. Heaven meant the world to them. They'd waited so long and prayed so hard for a baby. To look at her now, just shy of two years old, they still couldn't believe how quickly time had flown by. As parents, Quinn and Andre learned so much about life through the eyes of a child. Heaven only saw the good in life. She held no grudges and never stayed upset for too long. She forgave quickly, laughed often, and found the greatest joy in the simplest things. There weren't any emotional judgments, and no history fogged her vision. Quinn felt like she'd been failing countlessly as a mother. Her condo was always in a constant state of chaos, and she often washed the same load of laundry three times. She spent most of her days running late for work or tired from being up all hours of the night rocking and feeding a fussy baby, a sick baby, or a baby who just refused to close her little eyes. During bad dreams, Heaven rang out cries that sent Quinn running into door frames and across baby doll minefields. Her nights were restless and her present days felt like extensions of the day before and the day before that. As Heaven grew and got into daycare, Quinn had visited doctor's offices so often she felt like she should've had her own reserved parking spot. Sometimes she ran out of diapers, or the milk had gone bad, or her patience had worn thin from repeating requests to her demanding toddler for the hundredth time. As a woman, Quinn felt like she wasn't so good in that area either. Sometimes, everything in her life had gone wrong, and nothing seemed fixable; she didn't know how she would make it, but she kept going because there were no other options, and if she became undone then everything and everyone else would come unraveled with her. Many times, Quinn wanted to scream when she read words that told her to cherish these moments. The moments of pure exhaustion when she hung on by a thread. When she didn't remember the last time she had a proper meal or felt like she wasn't in charge of everything. When her heart wasn't torn by the guilt of craving a moment to herself while knowing that she should appreciate the gift of having a family to love. Throughout her season of turmoil in the fight for love, Quinn found that she'd done some *crazy* things. She killed a woman, and then nearly killed herself right in front of her daughter. What a selfish act it would've been to rob her daughter of an irreplaceable relationship, but for love, Quinn was willing to risk it all. Did it make her a bad person? No. It made her human. Tears of guilt fell from Quinn's stormy gray eyes as she reminisced on the humanity of another woman; *her mother.*

"What's the matter, baby?" Andre noticed her tears.

"Just thinking," She looked up in regret. "You know, I think a walk in the park may be nice."

"Absolutely," he replied, wiping her tears. Quinn made breakfast while Andre played with Heaven. After they'd eaten and showered, they all took a walk to the park. They sat on a nearby Park bench watching Heaven chase the birds and play on the jungle gym. As they sat, Quinn poured her heart out to her husband. She told him the story of her mother and Ms. Sophia, how she met Diamond, and who was *really* involved in Pandora's kidnapping and escape. Andre stared in stunned surprise, allowing various emotions to wash over him.

"This is nuts," he shook his head. "Have you told Anna?"

"I did," Quinn nodded softly. "I didn't know if after all these years of holding it in she'd still look at me the same, but it didn't change her heart. She thanked me for being a loyal friend, and cried all over again about my mother."

"I can't even imagine," Andre looked flustered. "Surprisingly, Anna's tears weren't from anger, but mine was. For *years* I was angry at my mom for what she did, and I refused to forgive her. But Anna, she was proud of her. She applauded her for her brave heart and the boldness to do whatever was necessary for the love she thought she deserved. She was mortified that my mother died because of guilt and shame. She was hurt that she died alone and gruesomely," Quinn choked on her emotions, remembering the last conversation she had with her mother at the Pizzeria. "She died because I hated her and judged her for something she never intended to go so dangerously far. If I'd forgiven her that night, she'd still be here."

"Don't put that burden on yourself," Andre wrapped an arm around her. "You were seventeen years old and reacted as such. That was a lot to see and a whole lot to handle."

"It *was* a lot to handle," Quinn admitted, "and I just wish I was mature enough to have handled things differently. I loved my mom so much growing up. She was like my idol, and I wanted to be just like her. She was gorgeous, brilliant, rich, and everyone loved her," Quinn smiled, reminiscing. "She had a beautiful heart and a soft spot for me. I remember going everywhere with her, and everywhere we went, the world loved her. I went through life thinking she was flawless and unbreakable. And then I discovered her humanity. It was awful and dirty, but it wasn't who she was. I defined her by the mistakes she made instead of realizing she was a real human being that cried, failed, worried, and couldn't fix everything."

"Baby, sometimes we learn the most valuable lessons in the absence of our parents rather than their presence. Their mistakes teach us what not to do and help us to grow in some important areas in our lives," Andre dried the rest of Quinn's tears. "Your mom loved you. Use that same love to love Heaven. Teach her all the lessons you missed at seventeen. Be there for all of her important milestones in life, and work hard to be true to yourself, flaws and all." Quinn looked at Heaven, and a warm smile spread across her face.

'My mom would've been so in love with her."

"She would've," Andre agreed, "my parents as

well. They would've enjoyed being grandparents." Biting his lip nervously, he turned to face Quinn. "What do you think of trying for another baby?"

"I've thought about it," Quinn looked back at him. "I grew up pretty lonely, as did you. The one thing I always wanted aside from love and loyalty was a sibling."

"Ditto," He nodded, "I want a son *so* bad. You know Deacon Bailey just had a little boy."

"Did he?" Quinn smiled, "That's amazing. I didn't know his wife was pregnant."

"I'm not sure *she* knew either until she was pretty far along. I miss seeing you pregnant," he grabbed Quinn's hand and kissed it. "You were gorgeous. I regret that you went through most of it depressed because of me."

"I wasn't depressed the entire time."

"Not the entire time, but sixty percent of it," he gazed in her eyes. "We prayed and prayed for a baby and went through years of trying. When God finally gave us a shot, our situations ruined it. Let's have a do-over. Let's have another baby, buy another house, renew our vows- let's relive every moment that's been destroyed.

"Well with all the sticking and moving we've done in the last forty-eight hours, you just might get your wish," Quinn grinned. Andre's eyes widened.

"You're not on birth control?"

"For what? We were separated."

"Wow. I sure hope you are. I've been praying for our future"

"Well..." Quinn narrowed her eyes, "before we get to the future, there are some more things I think you should know about the past."

"Alright," Andre linked his hands with hers. "But, before we do let's promise to remember that this stuff *is* in the past. I don't mind venting about it, but we have to promise not to get angry or react in a way that would make the other person feel judged or ashamed."

"That's fair."

"Good," Andre replied. "I'd like to openly discuss what happened in college with Anna and Bruce. I really miss his friendship, and it's bothersome that I can't be there to see him, and Anna live out their dreams. Maybe all of us can get together at the beach house soon. If they allow it," Andre peered nervously at Quinn.

"I'm sure they would. I did mention pieces of your situation to Eden and Anna, but the honest truth should come from you. I'll call her and see if they'd like to meet up in the next few weeks."

"Good. We should also meet up with Desiree," Andre said. "Well, Diamond. Whatever she goes by." Quinn's heart nearly stopped.

"What?"

"Yes. I had no idea she was the granddaughter of the Perkins' or that you two knew each other. She and I had a situation, and I'm not sure exactly when or how, but then *you* and her had a situation, and we need to talk about it."

"We didn't have a *situation*," Quinn denied, "our marriage was rocky, I was vulnerable, and she was there. I got caught up in the moment and we kissed,"

Quinn looked down, embarrassed, "that was it. I had no idea she would-"

"Well let's talk to her together and clear the air. She's still a member of our church, and as leaders, we owe her some closure. I tried reaching out to her a few weeks ago to clear the air myself."

"Oh?" Quinn looked surprised.

"Yeah. I tried calling her, but her phone keeps going to voicemail. I went to her house, but apparently, the neighbors said she hadn't been home in a while. They think she may have gone back to Texas, but her car was still in the church parking lot amongst all the rubble. I believe someone tried reaching out to her to move it, but she never responded."

"Desiree is dead," Quinn replied flatly. She briefly thought of a more emotional way to say it, but nothing came to mind other than to spit out the cold hard truth.

"Dead?" Andre's eyes widened like saucers. "Are you sure?"

"I'm sure," Quinn swallowed. "...I killed her." Andre popped up from the park bench like popcorn."

"Mannequin..." He looked horrified.

"Wait a minute, you *did* just promise not to react in a way that would make me feel judged," She reiterated, folding her arms. Andre's expression turned blank and his mouth fell open.

Chapter 13

Doctor, are you feeling okay?

Two years ago…

Opening the door to her office building, Quinn walked down the long corridor. Her secretary, Rosa, followed briskly behind looking at Quinn's schedule in disbelief at how behind she was.

"Dr. Bentley, where on *earth* have you been all week? We've been calling and emailing you. I was prepared to send out a missing persons report by tomorrow."

Good morning, Rosa," Quinn ignored her questions. "I'm here now. What's the damage?"

"Well, your temporary hiatus has you overbooked for the rest of the month," Rosa shook her head, "and don't expect any lunch breaks for the next three months."

"I don't think I've ever had a solid lunch break anyway," Quinn chuckled, "What's on the schedule for today?"

"You have Sarah at ten a.m. Do you remember her?"

"Sarah...Sarah," Quinn searched her brain until she landed upon a face. "Oh yes, Sarah. The one with the temper the size of Texas."

"Yes, well now she's worried about her four-year-old daughter. You've made such great strides with

Sarah; she wants to know if you could potentially take on little Chelsea."

"Children aren't really my expertise. I'm not sure if I'd be the right fit. Can we pass her off to Dr. Smith's office?"

"I tried," Rosa huffed, "she requested you and refused any other recommendations."

"Well alright, I'll see what I can do then. Squeeze her in for sometime next month."

"Okey dokey," Rosa glanced down at Quinn's crowded schedule book with an attitude. She hated that Quinn was always so nice and could never say no to anyone. There were twenty-three psychologists in Virginia Beach, but Quinn was the most effective and the most popular. Making a decision to see a psychologist was a hard pill to swallow for some. Many people found it frightening to share their deepest secrets and struggles with a stranger, but with Quinn, building trust came easy. In being the First Lady of Tabernacle Church of God in Christ, people all over the country knew who she was. They fell in love with her brimming enthusiasm, hospitable demeanor, and warm smile. She was the golden girl of Virginia Beach. She was a beautiful and charismatic motivational speaker, a budding author, and a good friend. She had an elusive personality filled with grace, poise, and class. She was always soft-spoken, but her words could cut through metal. The world was a very demanding and stressful place to live in, so it was no secret why there were always patients groveling at the office door of a therapist. People needed help. They had questions and wanted answers. And they wanted them from Quinn.

"At eleven you have Joe, the one with the panic attacks. His doctor took him off the Ativan because he was becoming dependent on them, and now his attacks are worsening."

"Okay."

"At noon you see Bill and Megan. They need advice on how to deal with their fifteen-year-old son. He smokes pot, parties often, doesn't listen to his parents, and skips school."

"Sounds like a normal teenager to me," Quinn chuckled, walking through her office door. She sat down at her desk and sifted through what looked like an endless stack of paperwork."

"At three, you have Tasty."

"Tasty?" Quinn looked up, confused.

"Tasty is her stage name," Rosa hid her grin, handing Quinn a folder. "Her true alias is Desiree. She was a Pastor's wife over at Bethany down in Texas, and then moved here to pursue a career in stripping." Quinn blinked rapidly, staring at the folder. *A First Lady turned stripper?*

"This should be fun," Quinn skimmed through the file.

"From three forty-five until seven you have two new clients, a meeting with the staff about our annual luncheon, and a meeting with the department manager to discuss bills and look over the accounts.

"Sounds like a plan, thank you, Rosa," Quinn offered a warm smile.

"Oh, also, the CEO of the Wilson Firm is on line three. She wants to see how the building expansion project is going."

"Building Expansion project?" Quinn looked at Rosa, "I never gave the go-ahead to do any expanding, I'm still trying to decide if we have the money to do it."

Rosa pursed her lips," Line three, Dr. Bentley," she smirked before turning to walk out. Quinn was always modest and content where she was. She treaded lightly over the idea of expanding her business and hiring more staff. Rosa had been begging her to do so for years, but she'd always politely shut her down.

"I did not agree to any building expansion project," Quinn picked up the phone and fussed into it with an attitude.

"Good morning, sunshine," An enthused Pandora sounded from the other end. "How are you?"

"I'm sorry," Quinn adjusted her tone. "Good morning. Now," she turned her attitude back on, "*who* do you think you are to go over my head and-"

"I didn't go over your head," Pandora rebutted, "are you aware that you have one hundred and fifty-two clients and are only *one* person?"

"I'm fully aware," Quinn replied. "It gets a bit hectic from time to time, but God gives me the mental stability to handle it."

"God also gives you common sense. That's insane. *You* are overworked, *your* poorly staffed Suzy homemaker of an administration is overworked, and you're bursting out of your hole in the wall office," Pandora fussed. "Your accountant sent me copies of your books. You make over three hundred thousand dollars a year, and you've never even cut yourself a *paycheck.* What the hell is wrong with you?"

"Nothing," Quinn defended. "I get paid enough from the church and don't need it. Whatever I make here I always put it back into the business for a rainy day."

"Okay, well you've accrued four million dollars over the last six years for a rainy day. It's time to do something with it. As much as you would like to help one hundred and fifty-two people and *counting*, you cannot. You need to hire a staff of good therapists, and you need a bigger building. I set you up with a meeting at Value Options to talk about a new contract and see what they have to offer as far as new employees are concerned."

"Value options? Anna, that's a *big* company. I can't go in there alone. I'd need a lawyer present to overlook the contract and to draft-" Quinn paused, remembering she was on the phone with one of the best lawyers in the country. Although Pandora was a criminal lawyer, she knew enough about business to make any situation work. And because they were friends, Pandora wouldn't dare charge her a dime for her services. Quinn thought about her business for a brief moment. It *was* growing rapidly, and while she hadn't looked at her accounts in months, she was certain she'd made a killing. Quinn played around with the idea of expanding, but the thought of scheduling meetings to see how much she could afford and doing interviews to view potential new hires seemed too hectic. Besides, her mind had been wrapped up in her troubled marriage over the last six months. Rosa didn't forget, however, and while she wasn't brave enough to tell her boss to grow some balls and get moving, she reached out to Quinn's best friend who owned a *big* set of her own that could get the job done.

"I'll see you at six-thirty tonight?" Pandora replied sweetly.

"Alright," Quinn agreed, "six-thirty it is."

"Great. I'm excited for you!" Pandora squealed.

"Yeah-yeah. I see Rosa got you to do all the dirty work," she giggled.

"I'm glad she did. What is going on over there? It's not like you work in such a tacky environment."

"Tacky?" Quinn raised an eyebrow, offended.

"Honey, you communicate with your staff via walkie talkie." Quinn thought about it for a split second before rolling her eyes. She knew Pandora was right.

"Rosa also said you were out all week. Are you alright?"

"Yeah," Quinn lied, "I've just been home dealing with church stuff. I was up until about four a.m this morning. I almost didn't make it in today."

"Join the club. I'm working on a big murder case. Some guy shot up a convenience store and slaughtered the owner and his wife over a bottle of soda. I've been working on getting him off on temporary insanity, but this is a hard one. I haven't been able to sleep in days."

"I see Isaiah 42:28 holds true; *There is no rest for the wicked*," Quinn shook her head. Pandora laughed, as they briefly went on to discuss their busy workday, the details of the Value Options meeting, and a girl's night they should plan soon. Although Quinn was backed up with work, hearing her best friend's voice put her mind at ease. After hanging up, she spent the next four hours fixing her client's lives. Between sessions, she caught herself up on paperwork and responded to emails. Periodically, she stared at the photo of her and her husband on her desk and fought her emotions to hold back tears. Her marriage had always been on good terms, but now, Quinn didn't know what was going on anymore. Andre was short with her, stayed out late, and left early. He barely responded to her texts, sent her straight to voicemail when she called and was always irritated with her. He wouldn't look at her when he talked to her, and they hadn't made love in almost three weeks. It was like she'd done something to him, but she couldn't figure out what. She stayed up half the night thinking about it and woke up depressed the next day. She couldn't pick herself up to go to work, eat a good meal, or reach out to her friends. Quinn felt so sick, but she knew she couldn't stay in the house crying another day, so she decided to come back to work. As she navigated through her workday, she regretted it. She crawled through appointment after appointment hanging on by a thread, listening to her clients talk about their never-ending litany of problems. *My parents are mad at me. My mother hates me. Life isn't worth living. I'm a failure. I'm impotent. On the way over here I felt like driving my car into a telephone pole. I'll never be happy. No one understands me. I don't know who I am. I hate my job. I hate my life. I hate you.*

After her two-thirty appointment, Quinn rushed outside to get some fresh air, but she was met with the mailman who stopped her to talk about *his* problems. It took every ounce of superhuman strength she had to listen to him moan about his lousy marriage for fifteen minutes. When she turned to come back into the building, she noticed a happily married couple walk past holding hands. They smiled at one another, snuck in a few kisses, and talked about the right time to have children. This sent Quinn's emotions over the edge.

Rushing back into the building, she high tailed it to her office, closed her door and began to cry. She was depressed and tired of pretending to be happy. She had so much to say and not a soul to say it too.

"I guess it's true about therapists being crazier than their patients," she thought.

"Good afternoon," A woman's voice entered her office. A stunned Quinn wiped away the cascade of tears falling from her eyes before turning around.

"Hi," she sniffed, putting her game face back on. "Can I help you?"

"I'm Tasty," the woman looked at Quinn concerned, "Are you alright?"

"I'm- yes," Quinn replied, a bit taken aback. She peered out the door looking for her secretary. "Did someone send you back here?"

"Oh, no. I didn't see anyone at the reception desk, so I walked back myself. I'm sorry. Is there a waiting room I should go sit in until you're ready?"

"Um," Quinn looked at the woman's file. She usually took fifteen minutes to look over her client's cases before she welcomed them in, but Tasty was already inside. Quinn didn't have the concentration to sift through the file anyway, so it didn't matter at this point. "No, it's fine," she stood up. "I'm Dr. Bentley; it's nice to meet you."

"Tasty," the woman replied.

"Have a seat," Quinn gestured for the woman to sit wherever she wanted. "There's a chair if you'd like to talk Doctor to patient, or there's a couch if you'd prefer a more relaxed situation."

"It's been a long day of traveling on trains and uncomfortable chairs," Tasty laughed, "I think I'll take the sofa."

Quinn looked down at her file to remember her name, "Desiree, is it?"

"Yes, ma'am."

"What brings you into counseling?"

"Life," Tasty shook her head. "I've made such horrible choices in the last year. At first, I was okay with it, but the deeper I get, the more convicted I feel. I'm ashamed, I'm embarrassed, and can't even remember what dignity feels like anymore. I asked my insurance company to point me to the best person that could help me, and they sent me here."

"I'll do my best," Quinn smiled. "Your file says you were the First Lady of Bethany Baptist in Texas," Quinn looked at her notes and then peered up at Diamond, confused. "My husband preached there last year, I believe. Your ex-husband seemed like a fine man. What happened?"

"He is a *fine* man," Tasty sneered, "too fine for his own good. We met here in Virginia when I was a teenager. He's from Texas but came down for the summer to visit his grandparents. I haven't had the best memories here in Virginia Beach, so when Jeff and I got serious, I moved out there with him."

"Oh, so you're from Virginia Beach?" Quinn asked. "I thought you were from Texas."

"I was born in Texas," Tasty confirmed. "My father is in the Army, so we moved around a lot. I moved to Virginia Beach when I was two years old. My father was always in and out with the Reserves, and my mother worked a lot too, so they left me with my grandparents. My grandfather molested me for a good majority of my childhood here, and it took me years to recover from it. So as I said, when Jeff and I got serious, it felt good to get away."

"I understand," Quinn nodded.

"Anyhow, we had a pretty good marriage, and then one day he changed. He started to ignore me and treat me badly. As the First Lady of a church, I was often the one most women looked up to. I didn't have very many friends but the ones I did have, I was the main source of support for them. Needless to say, when my marriage started to fall apart, I didn't have anyone to talk to. I felt alone, angry, and depressed." Quinn felt herself becoming misty-eyed. *Tasty's story sounded all too familiar*. She blinked quickly, trying to control her emotions. "Eventually I found out that Jeff had cheated on me with multiple women. I confronted him, and he divorced me. I signed a prenup when we got married, so when he divorced me, he left me alone, homeless and broke.

"I'm so sorry," Quinn shook head remorsefully.

"I was so distraught and desperate to get out of Texas that I slept with a few old men to earn enough money for a plane ticket," Tasty bit her lip, embarrassed. "I chose old men because they were familiar, considering my past. I flew back to Virginia Beach and stayed a few nights in a Women's shelter. It was there that I remembered the voice of my grandfather. I'm not sure if you remember the story of the Perkins case, but he was a sick man. He molested young girls and killed them. One in particular, he kept in the basement." Quinn furrowed. "He would've killed *her,* but she had a friend who was super determined to get her out. My grandfather told me a long time ago that I would never amount to anything other than a whore, but that girl who helped me break free a long time ago, she made me feel like I could live a normal life despite what had happened to me and I believed her. I took her words and flew all the way to Texas." Quinn's lips parted as a vague sense of familiarity washed over her. "But when my ex-husband did what he did to me, and I found myself at a night club stripping for money, all I could hear was my grandfather's voice reminding me of my true worth."

"Diamond?" Quinn stood up in shock. Diamond looked up at Quinn and immediately, it was as if the same deja vu hit her too.

"Quinn!" her eyes widened.

Quinn and Diamond stared at one another for a long time, the secrets of their emotional past filling Quinn's office like smoke. After that session, Diamond became a top priority for Quinn, and she went above and beyond her call of duty to help her. She worked tirelessly to help Diamond sort out her issues and regain her self confidence. She got Diamond a job at a nearby hotel, which gave her a place to stay and a feasible income to buy food and other necessities. Quinn also invited Diamond to church and reintroduced her to God. After six months of progress, Diamond felt like a brand new woman and cut her therapy sessions off. Shortly after, she reached out to Quinn to have lunch. Now that therapy was over, Diamond wanted a friend. Quinn didn't usually intertwine her patient-therapist relationships, but Desiree was different. While it was true that Quinn helped *her*, Diamond also helped Quinn escape the emotional turmoil of her broken marriage. During this time, Andre's attitude had gotten significantly worse; so bad that one night Quinn left the house and went to the hotel where Diamond stayed. It wasn't like her to talk to anyone about her personal issues; *especially her marriage*. Some of the things that went on in her life she hadn't even shared with Eden and Pandora. But Diamond understood. As a former Pastor's wife, Diamond was relatable and easy to talk to. Quinn told Diamond about her marriage troubles and her confusion with it all. Diamond observed Andre in church and knew *exactly* what his problem was. As a former stripper, Diamond could spot a weak-minded, cheating husband anywhere. The second she walked into the church, she could feel Andre's eyes on her body. Diamond knew the kind of man Andre was and began to feel bad for Quinn. *She also began to fall in love with her.* As a stripper, Diamond had done a number of provocative things to men and women alike. She never considered herself to be a lesbian or a bisexual, but she appreciated the figure of a beautiful woman. She also slept with them from time to time when she wanted the kind of closeness and intimacy she couldn't get from a man, but *falling in love with a woman was out of the question*. When it came to matters of her heart, Diamond was strictly dickly. *She loved men*, but something shifted after becoming friends with Quinn. They began to text and talk more often, and sometimes Quinn stayed nights in Diamond's hotel room when her husband was away on preaching engagements and didn't want her to travel with him. Without warning, Diamond started to notice different things about Quinn- how her clothes hugged her body, how her gorgeous gray eyes framed her face, and how her innocent voice filled a room. Still, Diamond's mind focused on men. All men. *Always* men.

Then, her heart shifted. Diamond couldn't pinpoint if it was the fact that they were both lonely, or that they were always together, but the more Quinn's marital life deteriorated, Diamond found herself constantly around to pick up her broken pieces. She'd get excited when Quinn texted her or came by to see her. Diamond's Facebook wall was dominated by articles and pictures that reminded her of Quinn, and soon Quinn was everywhere she looked. Thoughts of Quinn filled every quiet moment. She constantly replayed conversations they'd had and envisioned future ones. Quinn's beautiful face appeared in the black beneath Diamond's eyelids as she drifted into slumber, and she subconsciously reached for Quinn next to her each morning as she slowly reopened them. Pretty soon, it became all Quinn. *Always Quinn.* Diamond *had* to have her, and she *had* to know if Quinn felt the same way. After mustering up the courage, she decided to ask her. The next day, Diamond blew Quinn's phone up with calls and text messages begging her to come over so she could pop the question. Quinn had already had a busy day at work and would soon have to go home to more hell from Andre. Diamond's constant phone calls and text messages started to annoy her. A few months prior, Quinn noticed Diamond becoming really pushy. She seemed to get emotional when Quinn told her she couldn't come by, and jealous when she couldn't spend every waking moment with her because she was out with Eden and Pandora or swamped with work. Quinn knew their friendship was important to Diamond, and she wanted to be there for her, but Diamond's reactions to certain things started to bother her. After Diamond's fifteenth text message, Quinn decided to go over to see what

Diamond wanted. She also decided it was time to tell Diamond how uncomfortable her behavior was starting to become, and that maybe it was time for her to step back. After work, Quinn got into her car and drove to Diamond's house. On the way, she received a phone call from her annoyed husband about the upcoming women's retreat and how much he needed her to be there. After the way they fought and argued that morning, running a women's retreat was the last thing on her mind. But even though she was upset with her husband, she couldn't leave the women at church without their First Lady.

"I can't stay long, I have to run home and get dressed for church tonight," Quinn walked into Diamond's hotel when she opened the door.

"I thought you said you weren't going to church because you had work to do," Diamond looked at her.

"I wasn't, but the women's retreat slipped my mind. It's been relocated, and Andre wants me there to relay the details.

"Well, I thought we could stay here and hang out," Diamond followed Quinn into her mini kitchen.

"I'm sorry, I don't have time today. I'm super busy."

"Is you being busy the reason you keep ignoring my phone calls?"

"I'm not ignoring them on purpose, I just have a ton of work to get done and don't have my phone with me all day."

"But you responded to your husband's phone call."

"Yes, but-" Quinn winced, catching herself. "Wait, excuse me?"

"Nothing, forget it," Diamond rolled her jealous eyes.

"Diamond, we need to talk," Quinn sighed, "What is with your pushy wa-" Diamond leaned into Quinn and kissed her.

With widened eyes, Quinn snatched away and stepped back.

"I love you," Diamond stared at Quinn, lifelessly. "I don't know when, or why, or how, but I love you." Quinn watched Diamond in a state of shock. Suddenly, all kinds of red flags began to rise. Had she been unknowingly leading Diamond on *all* this time? *The late-night text messages. The sleepovers*. Had Diamond been taking Quinn's friendship as something more than what it was? Quinn's speechlessness left the door open for Diamond to dive in for a more intimate kiss. Before Quinn could gather her thoughts, Diamond pushed Quinn into the wall and kissed her lips a second time. *And Quinn didn't stop her. What was she doing?* Quinn was far from a lesbian and far from being bisexual. How was this happening? What doors did she leave open? And again, *why couldn't she stop herself?* Diamond wrapped her arms around Quinn's waist and pulled herself closer as they made out for almost ten minutes. As a beautiful therapist, Quinn was often the object of her male patient's desires, but she maintained a professional boundary *all the time*. The therapeutic relationship is a special one. It is characterized by *exceptional* vulnerability and trust that Quinn made her business *not* to cross. However, reality sank in as Diamond slid her hands up Quinn's shirt that it wasn't Diamond who'd been the vulnerable one. *It was her.* When any relationship goes into the doldrums and creates distance between a couple, an affair always becomes a possibility — especially when attention is given to a woman who is lonely and in desperate need of being heard and appreciated. In her broken and depressed season, Quinn left her door of vulnerability wide open. Since she never entertained the possibility of an affair with another man, the devil decided to masquerade himself and *strut* through the door instead– high heels and all. Satan is cunning, smart, conniving, and all he ever needs to sabotage the promises of God in our lives is an *open door*. With every ounce of will power she had left, Quinn pushed herself back and panicked.

"We have to stop," the edge in her voice set off all types of Alarms.

"Stop?" Diamond tried moving closer. "But you lik-"

Quinn stepped back again, breathing heavily.

"Stay back and stay away," she threatened.

"Mannequin you loved it, and you love me too. You and I both know your husband doesn't deserve you. He's a lying, cheating bastard just like mine."

"*Yours* proved it. Mine didn't. *At least not yet.*"

"Seriously?" Diamond winced, "If I wanted to, I could turn him out with very little effort, in the comfort of your *own* house," she sneered, "and I'd call you in mid-stroke just to prove it."

"Diamond," Quinn pointed, still trying to ward off the shock of her lips touching another woman. "I'm serious. I like you as a friend, nothing more. This can't happen again, and I don't think we should be friends anymore."

"What?" Diamond furrowed, her eyes

immediately filled with tears, "Are you serious? Wh-"

"I have to go," Quinn quickly turned on her heels and rushed out of Diamond's hotel. She hurried to her car and pulled off as quickly as she could. Part of her was so angry at herself for allowing things to get this far. If her marriage wasn't broken then, it was certainly broken *now*.

Later that evening…

Does anyone have any questions or concerns for me before we dismiss?"

"I do," Diamond, a stripper, turned born again believer sat in the front row with a white form-fitting dress that exposed her sun-kissed triple D cleavage, stood to her feet. "If all of our weekend activities are canceled, what about the woman's conference?"

"I believe that's still going on," he replied, "First Lady booked another venue. I'm sure she'll reach out to the committee as soon as things are finalized."

"Is she here at all?" Diamond asked with a mischievous grin, fluttering her eyes in a way that only Andre could notice. Diamond studied him. She'd been doing so very blatantly these days and realized she was beginning to become a distraction for him. As she flirted from her seat, Andre couldn't help but glance at her beautifully toned legs. She relaxed her body back into the wooden pew, her eyes locked on him as she crossed her legs to give him a better view.

"She had a previous engagement this afternoon," Andre cleared his throat. He hadn't spoken to Quinn all day, and he knew after the way they left one another this morning, there was no way Quinn would step foot in his presence.

"Well…Since the First Lady isn't here, I—"

"First Lady is right here," everyone in the room focused on the side stage door where Quinn had just entered. She walked in gracefully, yet confident. Her heels clicked on the hardwood floor as she walked to her seat on the pulpit.

Andre turned to her. He was shocked that she actually made it out. "Hi, Baby. You made it. We were just asking for you."

"Were you?" Quinn asked.

"Sister Diamond had questions about the women's conference this weekend, and wanted to know if it was still going on," he passed Quinn the microphone.

"Indeed, the conference is still on ladies," she smiled. "Since we can't use the church anymore, I was able to secure us a space at the Radisson Hotel in Richmond. If anyone needs a ride, there will be a bus leaving from the Church at three p.m sharp on Friday," she glared at Diamond. "Does that answer your question, *Sister Diamond*?" Quinn was far from oblivious of Diamond's hidden intentions. The poisonous stare she gave her let Diamond know she knew it.

"Yes…" Diamond replied dryly, "Thank you." Snickers from a few of the women could be heard throughout the room.

"Well then," Andre cut through the awkward silence. "I will see everyone here on Sunday. You're dismissed." The members got up from their seats and walked through different exits. Andre glanced to his left to see Diamond exiting the building. Her round buttocks stuck out like two volleyballs as she strutted to the door.

Instantly, he was aroused. Diamond swung her hips and pranced to the exit. She felt Andre's eyes all over her. It was almost *too* easy.

Eventually, Diamond got what she wanted. She slept with Quinn's husband, and as promised, she purposely pocket dialed Quinn in the midst to make sure she heard it.

Quinn cut off all communication with Diamond, promising to take their explicit encounter to the grave. Even after she and Andre resurrected their marriage, Quinn was too ashamed of it all and vowed to keep her secret. But we must be *careful* keeping secrets from our spouses. Satan often hides out in the darkest corners of our lives. According to the Bible, he prowls around like a lion looking for someone to devour, but many times he doesn't have to look very far. Diamond waited patiently for another weak moment to make a move. After the church bombing, she executed it a second time, putting Quinn's marriage in yet another bond. Know and understand that the same Devil who helps you conceal your secrets will eventually reveal them to your spouse. God ordained marriage as a part of *his* plan, as it is the building block of the body of Christ and society. God uses marriage to witness *his* glory. Marriage is the highest and most sacred covenant, the same as Jesus has with the church. We need to take seriously his offer; *Choose Life or Death.*

Chapter 14

"Take courage, I AM" –Matthew 14;27

4th of July weekend

Two weeks later, Quinn, Pandora, and Eden sat on the deck of their beach house with Andre and Bruce. The day was postcard perfect; even the buses were running on time. In downtown Virginia Beach, the sky was an unbroken backdrop of blue. The beach was a blaze of parasols and hot colors to match the burning sand underfoot. Against the percussion of the waves, laughter emerged in bursts, rolling like the ocean. Commuters walked like shoals of fish in a myriad of directions, after all, Virginia Beach was a renowned tourist attraction and was often visited this time of year. Tourists came from far and wide, grins wide and wallets wider. They packed out the beach and overcrowded the boardwalk, taking selfies and group pictures. Heat licked at their sunburned faces and coiled around their limbs like a hot-blooded serpent. The ground smoldered and sent up a disorientating haze. Seagulls frolicked about waiting for food to fall, and children screamed and hollered in their irritation of the heat.

"I hate to break up the beautiful mood," Bruce held Pandora in his lap, rubbing her belly, "But Ms. Sophia and Ms. Olivia were a real thing?"

"Bruce, I'm trying to be a supportive pastor and husband," Andre replied, amused.

"And the pastor in you wouldn't have *wanted* to be a fly on the wall in *that* room?" Bruce's eyes widened. Quinn and Pandora gasped. Turning to face her husband, Quinn folded her arms and darted her eyes.

"Baby, let's be real. Dr. Gray had legs for days, and you know it," Andre rubbed a hand down his face, trying his best not to burst into laughter as he sat in a lounge chair with Quinn beside him.

"And Miss. *Sophia*, with the side of Mac Titt—"

Pandora elbowed Bruce in the chest. He crumpled over into laughter.

"You guys are sick," Eden shook her head, amused at their immature entertainment.

"It's all love. We adore your mothers. They passed down all the good assets," Bruce flirted, moistening his lips before planting a kiss on Pandora's cheek.

"I'm just happy we can find some humor in it all," Eden said. "We've all been through a heck of a lot together."

"Touché," Quinn nodded in agreement. "Growing up, my mother always read me fairy tales. In it, there was always a handsome prince after a woman, and once they made it to one another, they lived-"

"*Happily ever after*," Everyone finished the sentence.

"Exactly. And as we grow up, we're fed false perceptions of what happily ever after looks like through television and social media. Little girls grow up believing in perfection and flawlessness, and as they transpire into adults, they carry those horrible misconceptions with them." Quinn said.

"And when their relationships get complicated, and all hell breaks loose, as it *always will*, they chicken out. Hence, the crazy divorce rates," Pandora stated. "And after the bitter divorce they go on to commit murder and conspiracies and come to me looking for help," She chuckled.

"It's a blessing that after everything we've gone through, here we are, still intact. The road wasn't as smooth as we may have liked but we learned some really valuable lessons. I took a bullet to the head in the name of love," Eden shook her head.

"And I battled a crazy addiction that almost destroyed me and my entire family, but I'm still here," Andre replied, "I still have my wife and my baby, and a new church…thanks to y*ou,"* he furrowed at Pandora. Pandora glanced up from the cupcake Eden handed her from her shopping bag.

"After what happened in college, I think we're even, brother," Pandora smirked through her devious glare. "Shall we declare a truce?"

"*No*. You're nuts," Andre looked at her like she was crazy.

"Nope," Pandora bit into her cupcake, "that crown has been passed on to your wife, honey."

"How about we snap the crown in half for you and Quinn to share it, because both of you are nuts," Eden looked at both of her friends.

"Agreed," Bruce chimed in. "Andre, remember when we were younger and chased after these girls? We all knew Anna was off her rocker, but Quinn? *Not Miss America*. I'm still in disbelief."

"What's disbelieving is you and Anna. *Happy*," Quinn smiled, looking at Bruce and Pandora nestled together, awaiting their first child.

"When's the wedding?" Andre grinned, "Tabernacle will be officially up and running by the new year. You two should be the first to get married there."

"I was thinking the same thing," Quinn said.

"I think we're comfortable with the way things are," Pandora stuffed her mouth full of cupcake. "Right Bruce?"

"Right," he agreed. Just as Pandora bit into her cupcake again, her teeth hit something hard. Immediately panicking, she quickly spit everything out of her mouth onto the floor and stood up.

"Ew," Eden jerked back.

"There's something in my cupcake," She looked down at the floor of the deck in disgust. Peering back at her was a big, shiny engagement ring. Her eyes clouded with confusion.

"I don't think he meant for her to spit it out like that," Andre whispered to Quinn, laughing to himself. Pandora turned to look at Bruce to see him on one knee. The look of disgust disappeared, and her mouth fell open.

"Bruce!" She hollered, fanning herself from the shock.

"You knew it was coming," he smiled, showing all thirty-two teeth as he knelt down on one knee and picked up the diamond. "After all these years, I finally have you where I want you: pregnant and in love with me," he slipped the ring on her finger. "You mean the world to me, and I want you for the rest of my life. You don't have to say yes just yet, I know-"

"Yes, yes! Oh my God, *yes*," Pandora smiled, practically throwing herself into his arms with a face full of tears. Everyone smiled at the beautiful scene. *After eighteen years, a long lost dream had come true.*

"You guys, this is so beautiful," Eden wiped her tears. "You deserve it."

"Were you all in on this?" Pandora cheesed, admiring the three-carat rock on her finger.

"Of course not," Quinn lied, "We've only known for about a month now."

"Congratulations you two," Andre gave a fist pump of appreciation, happy for his friends.

"Now all we need to do is get Heaven a sibling, and Eden a husband and kids, and our bucket list will be complete," Bruce implied.

"I agree to Heaven having a sibling," Pandora sat back down. "You and Andre need to get moving; she'll be two soon." Heaven played around on the deck steps with the sand. Quinn scooped her into her arms and sat her on her lap.

"Maybe we're already way ahead of you," She smirked as she and Andre held hands.

"*Shut up*," Eden's eyes widened.

"*Really?*" Pandora's hopeful eyes glistened. Andre reached into his pocket and pulled out the positive pregnancy test they'd taken the day before. The entire deck burst into screams, cheers, and excited laughter. *The beach house felt like Christmas in July.*

"I hope it's a boy this time," Bruce slapped Andre a high five. "My future quarterback needs a running back. How cool would it be to recreate our duo on the football field?"

"I hope so," Andre smiled at the thought.

"Hopefully your son runs faster than you."

"He will. As long as yours catches better than you," Andre joked.

"And for us, we already have Heaven, so if Quinn is

having another little girl, that makes two girls. If we can get Eden knocked up with a little girl, our little trio would live on," Pandora said.

"Well, if Quinn is having a girl then our little trio will be completed in about six months," Eden cheesed. "I'm pregnant." Everyone stopped talking.

"Excuse me?" Pandora grimaced in shock.

"I'm four months pregnant," Eden giggled.

"*With what*?" Quinn blinked in shock.

"Well it certainly can't be an animal," Eden replied, amused. "I've been trying to find a way to tell y'all for the last few months, but everyone was so invested in their own drama I figure I'd wait until things calmed down."

"Eden," Quinn put Heaven down and stood up. "*Pregnant?* You were doing so well in school."

"I'm still doing well in school, that hasn't changed. I graduate in four months."

"This is not okay, Eden," Pandora folded her arms

"Ladies," Bruce intervened, "She's *happy*. It's been a long time since she's had some good news to tell. Show some appreciation for her."

"Wait, no. I'm happy about the baby part. New life is always a blessing, but considering her selection of men, we have the right to be overbearing," Quinn defended.

"Damn right we do," Pandora fussed. "Who did you get pregnant by? I didn't even know you had a boyfriend."

"I d*on't* have a boyfriend," Eden confirmed. "I'm pregnant by my fiancé," she smiled, letting out another secret. "Oh, S*tephan*," she called. Stephan, the owner of Olives, waited in the house by the back door. Walking out to greet everyone, he smiled.

"You asked me a few weeks ago at Olives if you could meet my fiancé," Stephan smirked. "Eden, this is everyone. Everyone, *Eden."*

"Surprise," Eden smiled. Everyone stared at the couple as if they'd just produced a rhinoceros from their pocket. Eden could just imagine the sparks in their brains desperately trying to connect the dots, and instead just causing a short circuit. Pandora and Quinn looked like a pop-eyed toy from one of those claw machines at the fair. *Perfectly funny*, just as she'd imagined.

"Wow," Andre was speechless.

"How di- *wait.*" Pandora rubbed her temples. Quinn folded her arms, waiting for answers.

"Stephan and I have known each other since undergrad," Eden spilled the beans. "We dated all throughout freshman year."

"*This* is the guy you were telling us about in college?" Quinn asked, staring him down.

"That's me," Stephan smiled, taking in the awkward moment.

"I dumped him after I fell for Jackson. When I got back into my mother's shop full time, his mother kept trying to hook us back up. We've been seeing each other for the last six months. He asked me to marry him, and I said yes," she flashed the diamond on her hand that no one had even noticed.

"Holy crap," Pandora grabbed Eden's hand to stare at it.

"It's beautiful," Quinn furrowed in awe. Pandora gave Stephan a slow once over. Bruce pulled out his phone, and Andre stood up.

"Where are you from, boy?" Andre asked.

"I'm from Michigan," Stephan replied. "My mom and I moved down here while I was in school. I fell in love with Eden and wanted to stay here for good, but then we broke up, so I went back home after college." Quinn listened intently to Stephan as he spoke. She vaguely remembered him during Eden's first year at Virginia State.

"You guys are never happy for me," Eden huffed. She got up to walk away, but Quinn grabbed her arm.

"Honey wait, it's not that. I'm sorry. You know why we feel the way we do."

"I understand, but I'm grown," Eden shrugged. "Eventually, I'm gonna find my own happiness. Y'all spend so much time with your own families and lives that you don't realize *I'm a person too*. I look up to you guys, but I'm not living vicariously through you. I want *my* own happiness. Stephan makes me happy, and I've been wanting to tell everyone for so long, but nobody gives me a moment to say anything." Eden's eyes watered, and she started to cry. Pandora immediately felt bad.

"I'm sorry, Eden," She waddled over, extending a warm hug.

"I've heard a lot about you guys," Stephan said. "Eden's a great girl, and I love her. I'm not a bad guy. I'm not a murderer or a rapist, or an ex-con, or whatever else she's come across in the last few years. I'm just a club owner in love with a beautiful girl."

"He's clean," Bruce nodded, staring up from his phone. "Masters in Business, club owner, no children, no psycho ex-wives."

"Bruce, are you doing a background check on my fiancé?" Eden wiped her eyes, embarrassed.

"I am, baby girl. I'm still an FBI agent," he winked.

"I'm sorry I'm so uptight when it comes to you," Pandora smiled, "I'm happy for you, and I'm excited that we're all pregnant at the same time.

"Me too, this means *she*, or *he* won't be treated like

a tag-along because everyone will be around the same age," Eden smiled.

"Welcome to the family, good brother," Andre stood up, extending a handshake to Stephan.

"Thanks, man," Stephan smiled, "I appreciate it." As they all stood there and talked, a loud scream grabbed their attention. From the shock of everything that had transpired, everyone was too invested in their conversations to see Heaven walk down the deck stairs and onto the crowded beach. Onlookers screamed as the tiny toddler made her way into the ocean. They assumed she was with someone, but when she started to walk out too far, people grew frantic."

"Heaven!" Andre hollered. Everyone screamed and jumped up as paralyzing fear spread quickly throughout the beach. Andre and Bruce jumped the deck and raced to the water with the lifeguard. Quinn rushed down the steps screaming so loud her jaws locked and her throat nearly closed. Pandora waddled as best as she could down the steps, her heart throbbing in fear. Two lifeguards jumped into the water to grab Heaven, but it was too late. The ocean current snatched her up like a rag doll. Before anyone could reach her, she'd been washed out to sea. It was almost as if time began going in slow motion for Quinn. One second she saw her baby flying into the waves, and the next, she disappeared. She saw her husband and Bruce jumping into the water. She saw onlookers in a panic and lifeguards on their walkie talkies phoning for help. Time sped up, and Quinn raced to the ocean out of breath, as every cell in her body fought for oxygen. The ocean waves had begun to settle down, but there was no Heaven. Pandora tried running to the scene, but her belly began to wretch in an unbearable amount of pain. She fought with herself to keep running, but another surge stopped her. In those moments, for those seconds that seemed to stretch into infinity, there was nothing else. She fell to the ground and screamed.

"Anna!" A terrified Eden rushed over to her with tears rolling down her face. She was trying to get to Heaven, but now there was another Emergency. *Pandora had gone into labor...*

Two weeks later...

Bruce, Pandora, Eden, and Stephan stood in the living room of Quinn's condo at the repass after the funeral for their 1 ½-year-old daughter, Heaven. Quinn's home was filled with people Pandora and Eden didn't know. Somber strangers who were mostly dressed in black, walked around murmuring about how unexpected and unfortunate Heaven's sudden death had been, how shocking. Bruce, Eden, Stephan, and Pandora's heart broke for their friends as they avertedly listened to whispers of Heaven's name throughout the house. *No one had seen it coming. The Bentley's had overcome so much since the bombing of their beloved church. Heaven had been so young, so healthy. There were six people on the deck of the beach house and not one pair of eyes noticed her walk off? How would Quinn and Andre survive this?* All great questions and statements, Pandora thought as she walked through the formal living room picking up abandoned plates and cups. Eden trailed behind, clutching baby Bruce, Pandora's two-week-old newborn. Stephan and Bruce walked into the kitchen to load the dishwasher. The hospitality staff of Tabernacle offered to arrange for their staff to assist with cleanup and putting out the food, but Eden and Pandora said they would handle it because somehow the girls felt like helping in a time when there was genuinely nothing else to do. Rosa, who had introduced herself to everyone as Quinn's secretary, obviously felt the same way. Every fifteen minutes she carried a coffeepot throughout the room of mourners, offering refills. "Hey," Bruce walked up to Pandora and put his arm around her. "How are you holding up?"

"I'm alright, just wondering how we all get caught up in ridiculous tasks at a time like this. I can't stop cleaning up after people, Rosa is obsessed with the coffee, and you two are doing dishes."   Bruce squeezed his fiancée'.

"No one saw this coming."

"I just keep replaying everything over in my head," Pandora bit her lip, refusing to cry any more than she already had. "Was there something we could've done to prevent this? Was it our fault?"

"God, no. Heaven was a baby. Toddlers walk off, and it was just one of those things that we missed that ended in a freak accident." Pandora understood, but she doubted Quinn and Andre saw it that way. Pandora visually searched the room until she spotted Quinn standing by the window surrounded by a few members of her congregation. She was pale and seemed to have lost weight. Impossible, considering it had only been two weeks, yet she looked gaunt and drawn. Pandora saw that everyone else was talking, except Quinn. She stood in the middle of the group and yet, entirely alone. Her hands shook as she balanced a plate of uneaten food. The half sandwich and scoop of mac and cheese trembled. Andre walked the living room until it all became too much and he broke down and started to cry again. The congregation led him to the largest sofa as several guests moved to make room. The stress of everything couldn't be good for the baby Quinn carried, nor was the realization that her unborn child would never know their sibling. Was Quinn thinking that? Was she aware she was going to be a mother of one, *again*? Pandora thought about the agony and labor it took to birth little Bruce. She'd barely made it to the hospital on that fateful, yet, beautiful day. She screamed in agony in the ambulance. Most of it was her labor pains, and the other was for her God-baby whom she had no clue as to what had happened to her. By the time Pandora reached the emergency room, baby Bruce's head was already crowning, and she was ready to push. After fifteen minutes of ripping, tearing, screaming, and crying, she heard her son's cries. It was the most beautiful sound in the entire world. As she held the baby in her arms, she smiled at him but cried for Quinn. Pandora was excited and scared at the same time. Her blood pressure was up and down, and the doctors had eventually taken the baby and sedated her so she could rest. By the time she awoke, Bruce had broken the news that Heaven had drowned. Pandora cried for hours. She cried until there were no more tears left. How could this happen? She'd birthed a miracle, and her best friend had just lost one. *In the same hour.*   Little Bruce began to whine, signaling Pandora to reach for him. As she took him in her arms, she couldn't grasp what it must feel like to lose a living child. She'd gone through a lot in her lifetime, and even though pain was universal, Pandora's stomach twisted in knots thinking of what her friend was going through. She and Eden wanted to say something to their friend, to offer comfort. *A ridiculous need.* There was no comfort to offer. Andre and Quinn had just lost their baby. Heaven defined them. She'd made them parents. They lived their lives, planned their days, and interacted with the world, all of it as Heaven's parents. And now she was gone and they were expected to go on? *Impossible.*

"I feel so bad for her," tears fell from Eden's face. "I'm not sure how to articulate any of it."

"Me, too. It's horrible." Pandora shook her head. Eden touched her arm, then stepped away.

"I need to get back to my compulsive cleaning."

"Sure. I think we're gonna get going. It's time to put Bruce down for a nap," Pandora nodded, allowing herself a moment to savor the fact that she was a mother; that life was birthed through her and depended on her. She walked through the family room and picked up a few plates and cups, then returned to the kitchen. She walked over to Bruce, and the look in her eyes told him she was ready to go home. Bruce nodded and then walked over to Andre.

"We'll get through this, man." He reached in for a hug. Having to bury their baby was the hardest moment in Quinn and Andre's life. They spent their days praying, crying, and holding on to one another. Every night they drank a glass of wine to help them to get sleepy, but it didn't work. Andre was eventually able to sleep, but Quinn awoke every couple of hours to find herself crying. As the weeks passed, the fiery ache of missing Heaven never faded, never wavered. It was as constant as the rotation of the earth. The first week after Heaven's funeral had been different. People had been with Quinn and Andre all the time, guiding the rhythm of their now broken life. But one by one, they'd left. There were other things to be tended to, other places to be. Rosa had stayed the longest, but after four or five days, she, too, had returned home. Andre eventually went back to the church, but Quinn wasn't ready. She'd lost track of the days, and as her doorbell rang here and there, she didn't know if her visitor was as simple as the mailman or as complicated as anyone else. One day it rang, and she opened the door to see Pandora and Eden standing there, Pandora holding baby Bruce in her arms.

"You're not answering your phone," Pandora said by way of greeting. "That's going to get people worrying."

"I don't want to talk to anyone," Quinn admitted, trying to remember if she'd invited the two of them over. She didn't think so. "Why are y'all here?"

"Because we love you. Now let us in." Quinn stepped aside because it was easier. Eden rushed toward her and gave her the biggest hug. Although Quinn was still shattered, there was no way for her to tackle her days alone. She'd tried when she woke up in the mornings, but by noon she was shaking, and by three she was falling apart. If she *wanted* to wear a mask, she couldn't. *This was real life, and she needed to accept it.*

"Someone wants to say hello to you," Pandora smiled, unwrapping little Bruce from the blanket. Quinn instantly smiled. She washed her hands and took him into her arms. He was so tiny with the chubbiest cheeks and most beautiful chocolate skin. He looked like his father but had dimples like Pandora. The three of them sat on the floor together and played with him. For the first time, Quinn laughed and smiled more than she'd done in a while. Quinn knew losing her daughter was rough, but to look to her left and her right and see a best friend on each side, filled her with joy. She was pregnant, and although she and Andre were blessed to be having another baby, in a perfect world, Heaven would still be here.

"He's so beautiful," Quinn smiled at Bruce, a tear fell from her cheek.

"I had no idea motherhood was *this* hectic," Pandora sighed, "It took me two weeks just to get a good shower. I haven't slept more than three hours since I left the hospital."

"I remember those days," Quinn smiled warmly, "it gets better."

"When?"

"I'm not sure. I didn't sleep well until Heaven stayed nights with you. Telling me things got better is what people told me to make me feel better, and it gave me hope. I figure I'd tell you the same thing," she laughed.

"Bruce insisted we have a full-service nanny. He got hired as an FBI analyst, and he has to go out to Colorado for training for *six weeks*."

"Have you found anyone?" Eden asked. Pandora wrinkled her nose.

"A woman named Greta. She's worked with two people Bruce knows, and they speak very highly of her. She's in her early fifties, and she's never been married. She loves children, and whenever I'm around her, I feel inadequate." Quinn smiled.

"Stop it, Anna."

"No, I do." Pandora nodded, "she believes in a totally organic kitchen. She's a vegan but thinks meat is good for growing children. She bakes her own bread, does windows, and looks at me like I'm an idiot. Should I hire someone who intimidates me?" Eden giggled as Quinn checked her phone.

"How about we ditch Greta and I'll stay with you? Andre is getting ready to head to Florida for a few days for a men's conference. And then after that, he'll be in Buffalo for the Mission revival."

"Keeping himself busy?" Eden asked

"Yeah. That's his way of coping. He wanted me to go, but I really don't feel up to all the hassle. I could totally stay with you and help out."

"Are you sure? Because I would love that," Pandora smiled.

"I could stay, too. Stephan is super supportive of me being here for you guys. I don't think I could stay for the entire six weeks. I have finals at the end of the month. But I could certainly stay for two of them.

"It's a date," Pandora squealed. She wrapped an arm around Quinn, as Eden joined in from the other side. Reaching in, they planted a kiss on Quinn's cheek, causing her to form the biggest smile. Sometimes life was hard, and just when you least expect it, you have to start over. There was pain in that, but also satisfaction. With or without Quinn wanting it too, life moved on. Eden dealt with it, Pandora dealt with it, and she would, too. However, it didn't matter what season of life she found herself in, the loyalty of friendship *never* wavered.

Chapter 15

18 years later…

"Dad, I don't want to go to Clemson," eighteen-year-old Bruce glared at his father.

"BJ, you're a star running back that's just been invited to one of the *top* schools in the nation," Bruce Sr. fussed at his son. "This is a huge honor."

"It *is* a huge honor, just not for me."

"And it's a *full* scholarship, meaning, your mother and I can use the college fund we saved to buy a new house. *A kid-free one.*"

"I understand the honor it is to go to Clemson. I just want to go to Virginia State. Clemson is all the way in South Carolina. That's too far from home."

"You're eighteen. You don't *have* a home anymore. You will live at college."

"Whatever dad," BJ laughed, "Mom would kill you if you put me out. We all know who the *real* man of this house is," BJ grinned, proudly smirking. Bruce Sr. slapped him on the back the head.

"You'll be the man of the homeless shelter."

"One day you'll look back and be proud of me. I'm gonna follow your lead and go to Virginia State."

"We are officially Virginia State Trojans!" Andre Jr. barged into the beach house flashing his football scholarship.

"You got in!?" BJ's eyes widened at the paper. He leaped over the kitchen island and rushed over to Andre. They slapped high fives and performed their signature handshake.

"Jr, I'm *not* paying for you to go to Virginia State," Andre Sr. rushed into the beach house with an attitude. "You didn't even tell your mother and I that you applied."

"It was a surprise, dad. Besides, mom's a psychologist, I'm sure she knew anyway.

"Of course, because I thought we raised a good child that skipped the rebellious teenager stage," Quinn walked in behind them, dropping her luggage.

"I'm not rebellious," Andre Jr. declared. "I *never* said I was interested in Clemson just because they offered me a scholarship. Bruce and I wanted to do something on our own."

"Exactly," Bruce Jr. defended, "Listen, we just graduated high school, and y'all brought us to the beach house to celebrate, so let's celebrate. Us choosing to go to Virginia State shouldn't be a problem. At least we're *going* to college."

"Trojans!" Andre Jr. screamed

"Trojans!" Bruce Jr. joined in. Andre and Bruce Sr. watched their sons leap for joy, elated at their new journey.

"I hope both of y'all have money to pay for the Trojan tuition," Andre Sr. looked at Bruce Sr. "Can you believe them?"

"I honestly don't know where to put my anger," Bruce admitted, walking into the living room.

"I'm so confused. *What football player* wouldn't want to go to Clemson?" Quinn sat down on the couch. "

"Throw them out."

That last bit of advice was offered by Pandora, who

sat on the floor, stretching out her hamstrings. She looked up and shrugged. "They deserve to sleep in the street until they leave for college."

"That idea sounds lovely right about now," Andre murmured. He pictured his son laying on a cardboard box in the middle of summer, and it was more gratifying than it should have been.

"Were we *this* bad when we were younger?" Bruce Sr. added.

"Well, we did give up the same Clemson scholarship chasing behind women," Andre and Bruce looked at their wives.

"Hello everyone!" Eden's chipper voice filled the room as her and her husband Stephan walked in.

"Hey," they all muttered back.

"What's wrong?"

"BJ and Andre were awarded football scholarships to Clemson," Quinn replied.

"I remember you told me. That's exciting!"

"Well, at the last minute they declined the scholarships and applied to Virginia State behind our backs." Bruce huffed.

"Ha. I see history is repeating itself," Eden took a seat on the couch next to Stephan

"That was different, and you know it," Andre defended.

The six of them sat in the living room catching up with each other's lives. As they laughed and reminisced, it barely felt like eighteen years had gone by. Quinn, Pandora, Bruce, and Andre sank into their fifties like a favorite old armchair, while Eden and Stephan enjoyed the remaining years of their forties. They all felt like this age was where they were supposed to be. Reminiscing about their youth was always fun, but neither of them wished to go back there. Those were crazy times, *anxious times*, building a career and financing homes. The hectic life of raising toddlers had given way to the social whirl of teenagers, but in general, life had slowed to a more sedate pace. Andre and Quinn still served as the Pastor and First Lady of Tabernacle Church of God in Christ. It was still the largest megachurch in Virginia. Quinn was still a prominent psychologist whose business had become so popular, that she was requested all over the world to help others. After the death of Heaven, they were blessed two times over with a set of Twins, Peyton, and Andre Jr. They were still madly in love, and Andre still looked at Quinn like she was the most beautiful woman in the world. Together, they raised their children, traveled frequently and preached the Gospel. Quinn made it her business to be the best mother to her children as she could be. She loved her son but took extra pride in her daughter, Peyton. All the love she never got to give to Heaven, she gave it to Peyton. Days prior, she sat in the auditorium of Salem High School watching her twins graduate. She stood the entire time, clapping, crying and taking endless pictures. She screamed and held up congratulatory signs, blocking other people's views. Peyton was the valedictorian, on her way to Virginia State University to study Psychology. Quinn and Andre stood like proud parents, gleaming with joy.

"*Oftentimes we project false smiles of protection to hide our fears, to be desirable. We wear high heels and new clothes and carry certain bags and advertisements to show a sense of self, a projection, and an idea. We use extroversion to be well-liked. We chase "busy" to mask our fear of not leaving an impact. We cover a lot of things up;*

Scars we carry, stories we hold, work we're afraid of doing," Peyton stood at the podium, addressing her 1,100 classmates. *"Life is not a masquerade. It's important to always be our true selves. Before I take my seat, I want to thank my brilliant Mother, Mannequin Bentley, Ph.D. Thank you for the endless lessons that taught me to bring all of who I am to what I do, and that it's okay to be perfectly imperfect because It's the imperfections that make us who we are. Life is all about the journey, not the destination. So as we stand here as seniors, ready to take on the next ten years of our lives, may we always remember that in everything we do, to be real, to be honest, and to be us. Thank you."*

The entire graduating class leaped for joy, cheering and screaming. Quinn cheered and clapped with the biggest smile on her face. Andre wrapped an arm around his wife and smiled. Tears fell from Quinn's face as she stood present for a moment in her children's lives that her own parents had missed. She would've given a*nything* to have an emotionally present mother in her life, but she made sure to be one to her children.

"There's something magical about Peyton's mother," An onlooker watched Quinn.

"I was thinking the same thing. Look at her," Another parent replied. "She loves everything her daughter does. She praises her and makes jovial conversation. They have the kind of bond a civilization could be forged on just by following their example."

"I totally agree. I'd swap every possession I own to have a mother like that. I mean it."

The entire neighborhood had grown to love and cherish the Bentley's, and Quinn worked endlessly at her life to be certain that what was on display for the world to see was the exact same display taking place behind closed doors. The experience of life taught Quinn that when we wear masks, we carve a piece of ourselves out— withholding parts of ourselves as unworthy. But we can't truly be healed unless we offer up *all* the pieces. It's like handing someone a broken vase, asking them to fix it, but holding back two or three of the broken pieces. *Everything* in our lives gets cheated when we choose to hide behind masks. Pandora and Bruce got married, diving headfirst into parenthood and their new careers. Pandora enjoyed her new journey as a judge. Six months ago, she was asked to be a television judge for a major network. She was appalled. *The nerve* of the network to ask *her,* after years of hard work and schooling, to get on television and become *entertainment.*

"It's ridiculous," Pandora said firmly. "And I'm done having this conversation."

"What do you mean, it's super cool," Bruce Jr. told his mother. "Besides, you're getting old. People are going to stop taking you serious pretty soon."

"I'm fifty-two," she pointed out, trying not to let her annoyance bleed into her voice. Why on earth her husband and son couldn't let this go was beyond her. "I'm far from old."

"I said you're *getting* old. I broke my arm last year, and you were too busy complaining about me intervening on your soap operas to take care of me," he joked, "*That's* old." Pandora rolled her eyes.

"Are you really going to go there? Because we can talk about how I took care of you after you were circumcised." Bruce Jr. held up both hands in a gesture of surrender.

"Sorry, mom. I'll do anything if you don't talk about my penis." She relaxed. Order was restored, she thought happily.

"As long as you remember I have the ultimate power," she affirmed. "*I'm not old.*"

"Always and forever. You are the queen of this family, and we worship at your feet," Bruce Jr. playfully graveled.

"That's going a little far, but I accept your fealty." They were in the kitchen where all the important conversations took place. It had been a couple of weeks since Pandora's meeting with the network, and no one in the family was letting it go. She'd told Bruce, expecting him to be as shocked and outraged as she had been, but he'd told her she would make a great entertainment judge and should consider it. Forty-eight hours later, she'd still been openmouthed.

"It's less money and an insult to my intelligence," she reminded her son as she got up to get more ice cream.

"You and dad have like a billion dollars in the bank. You don't work for the money anymore. Mom, you could make a big difference. People love you. My friends love you. You're effective. Imagine the people you could reach on national television."

"I don't have the experience to be anyone's entertainment."

"You're selling yourself short." Just what her husband had said, she thought, both pleased and frustrated by her family's faith in her. Of course, Bruce Jr. was just like his Father. They were both over six feet with dark wavy hair and sun-kissed brown eyes. They were strong men with good heads and gentle hearts. The difference being Bruce Sr. had fallen in love with Pandora when they were young. Even though their love was off and on, Bruce Sr.'s relationships lasted for years at a time. Bruce Jr.'s idea of a long-term relationship was six weeks.

"Are you seeing anyone special?" Pandora asked as she returned to the table and handed him a bowl of ice cream.

"You know we don't talk about my love life."

"We don't talk about your sex life. There's a difference. Don't you want to fall in love?"

"Sure, one day, but for now variety is the spice of life."

"If you're worried about it getting boring with just one person, it doesn't have to. Sure there are times when things get routine, but there are also ways to break out of that. Your father and I still find each other exciting, and we've had sex at least a million times." Bruce Jr. froze, his spoon raised halfway to his mouth. The color left his face, and his eyes widened.

"Mom, stop. Honest to God, I would rather talk about my penis than this." Pandora's mouth twitched.

"I'm just trying to reassure you."

"I know, and it's great that you and Dad still do that kind of stuff, but I don't want to know. *Seriously*."

"All right. We'll talk about your penis instead." The spoon slammed into the ice cream bowl. Bruce Jr. sprang to his feet.

"I'm out of here." He circled the table and kissed her cheek.

"*We're still doing it like rabbits*," Pandora called after him.

"*I can't hear youuu*," The front door slammed shut. Pandora chuckled as she put Bruce's bowl in the dishwasher. Sometimes her kids were so easy to rattle it almost wasn't a sport. Bruce was the head of the FBI, and together, he and Pandora were a force to be reckoned with. In addition to eighteen-year-old Bruce, they also went on to have a daughter, eighteen-year-old Summer, nine months after Bruce was born. Pandora went from being infertile, to *extremely* fertile.

While it was a bit much becoming a mother of two within nine months of each other, Pandora accepted and reveled in it. She remembered the times she longed for a baby, and God had given her a *double* portion. She spent her life loving her children and being the best soccer mom, wife, and judge she could be. Eden and Stephan got married and traveled the world with one another. Both of them got into the business of buying houses and flipping them. They made so much of an income doing it, that neither of them needed to work a full-time job. Stephan kept his night club as an extra source of income, and they spent the next eighteen years caring for their daughter, seventeen-year-old Scarlet. Scarlet, Peyton, and Summer had been the best of friends. Their mothers raised them together, and they grew up doing much of the same things. Although everyone traveled and barely stayed in one spot throughout the year, they made it a family tradition to hold all celebratory events at their collective beach house. New Year's Day, Christmas, Easter, 4th of July, birthdays, and now, graduation, and vacations, all took place there. Everyone went outside on the deck to relax in the sun. Bruce Jr. and Andre raced across the sand tossing their football back and forth. Peyton, Scarlet, and Summer sat by the ocean in their bikini's fussing at the boys for kicking sand everywhere. The food hamper was packed with every good food imaginable, and the cooler was full of lemonade and beer. Andre and Bruce barbecued short ribs and chicken, and everyone played games and built sandcastles. Life had taken them around the world and back. Still, there was no place like 125 Beach House Rd.

"Did Bruce get in?" Peyton looked nervously at her friends.

"He did," Summer rolled her eyes. "You two are so obnoxious; it's sickening and cute at the same time."

"Did you tell your parents how you two have been sneaking around since you were thirteen?" Scarlet shook her head, amused.

"Of course not. I don't want them to know anything yet."

"Peyton, your mom is a psychologist, I'm sure she knows already," Summer reiterated.

"Know what? That you and BJ have been sneaking around since you were thirteen?" Quinn, Eden, and Pandora joined them in the sand.

"We didn't, but we do now," Pandora confirmed with a smirk. The three young girls gawked at their parents, totally embarrassed.

"Scarlet, you and your *loud*mouth," Peyton's face was red.

"How was *I* supposed to know they were gonna come creeping up behind us?"

"We're your mothers, ladies," Pandora laughed. "We would've figured it out eventually. Knowing this piece of important information, I can almost bet money that *you're* probably the reason my son gave up a full-ride scholarship to Clemson University," she playfully darted her eyes.

"Peyton?" Quinn folded her arms.

"Mom," Peyton pursed her lips and lowered her head. "Okay, yes. It's *sort* of my fault. I love him and don't want him to go so far away," A tear immediately fell from her face. Quinn and Pandora traded amused glances before Quinn slid an arm around her daughter. *The apple didn't fall too far from the tree.*

"Why are you crying?" Quinn asked.

"Because I feel like I'm ruining his life by asking him to stay, and I don't want to but I can't picture life without him and I wanted your opinion before he rejected Clemson but I realized I hadn't told you and I was scared to tell you or Anna because both of you would be upset and blame me for everything-"

"Whoa, take a breath why don't you," Eden rubbed her back to calm her down.

"I totally understand. I'm not upset. We were all young once, and we did the same thing. Although I was never good at hiding things from my parents. That was Anna," Quinn said.

"I can't believe you guys have been dating this *whole* time and never told us. How the hell have they been doing this right under our noses?" Pandora asked.

"Because you guys are getting old. You're not as sharp as you used to be," Summer joked.

"What is with you little *jerks* calling us old?" Pandora fussed. Eden and Quinn laughed.

"We are not old. We've been there and done that. If anything, we're seasoned," Quinn joked.

"Exactly. We know all too well about young girls and their little crushes," Eden chimed in.

"Crush is such an infantile word," Peyton stated. "One that must've been invented by people with an interest in belittling true love."

"What?" Quinn tilted her head.

"Bruce and I aren't *crushing*. I love him with the

passion hotter than a thousand suns. *He's the one*. His voice is like liquid adrenaline being injected right into my bloodstream. Every time I see him I get butterflies, no-*lions*- in my chest." Quinn felt her mouth drop open. *She was staring face to face with her younger self.* Pandora drew in a breath and laughed.

"You *can't* be serious," Pandora looked at Peyton like she was crazy.

"Welcome to our world, mom," Summer glanced at her watch. "It's barely two o'clock. Is it too early to make a Cosmo?"

"Excuse me?" Pandora looked at her daughter, horrified.

"In my defense, it's already five o'clock in New York and probably tomorrow in Australia," Summer responded innocently.

"Summer, you're not drinking alcohol. You're seventeen," Pandora hissed. In her irritation, Summer's actions reminded her of her younger self as well. She'd been drinking wine from her parent's cellar since she was twelve. Pandora made a mental note to check her wine cellar when they got back home to ensure her alcohol hadn't been tampered with. "Are you pregnant?"

"Pregnant?" Summer jerked her head back.

"Anna?" Eden laughed.

"What? I feel like I'm getting a taste of my own medicine at this point. I had to ask."

"We're all still virgins, thank you," Scarlet chimed in. "I'd be too scared to get pregnant anyway. One of my friends showed me an ultrasound photo, and It looked like she was carrying an alien instead of a human baby. I swear it had a lizard tail."

"Did she have sex with a lizard alien?" Eden

pursed. Scarlet rolled her eyes.

"Of course not."

"Then, unless her boyfriend has some very unusual relatives, you can let the lizard fears go." Eden patted her daughter's hand. She too, in mid-conversation, could see the dippy ways she once had instilled in her daughter. "Guys, this feels like deja vu."

"Oh my Goodness, I was getting ready to say the same thing," Quinn broke her stare. "How scary is this? I'm not sure I was as bad as Peyton though."

"Please, you were worse," Pandora implied.

"*Way worse*," Eden replied. "Peyton, I'm happy for you and Bruce. If you have a heart like your mother and he has the love and persistence of Big Bruce, you'll make it to forever. Whether he's in South Carolina at Clemson, or right next to you at State. Distance doesn't matter when it comes to true love."

"I know," Peyton agreed with a somber glow. "I guess it was selfish to talk him into staying."

"It's quite alright. As long as your mother pays his tuition, they'll be no hard feelings," Pandora implied.

"I'll pay the tuition. You pay for the wedding, and we'll go half on the grandkid," Quinn chuckled.

"*Grandkids*?" Peyton winced in disgust. "I don't want any weird-looking alien kids popping out of me."

"What is it *with* you young people and aliens? Is it a generational thing?" Eden asked the question so earnestly that Pandora and Quinn couldn't stop themselves from laughing.

"I love you girls so much," Quinn said easily, putting an arm around her best friends." Their daughters watched with smiles on their faces. They loved the closeness of their mothers. Through them, they learned the value of true friendship and loyalty.

"I agree, life with you two by my side has, and always will be an experience," Eden replied.

"You guys have been friends for so long. *Through everything.* We really admire that about y'all," Summer smiled.

"Yup," Pandora sighed. "We'll be friends until we're old and senile."

"And then we'll be new friends," Quinn said. They all burst into laughter.

THE END

Made in the USA
Columbia, SC
01 December 2020